THE SLEEPERS OF RORAIMA: A CARIB TRILOGY

AND

THE AGE OF THE RAINMAKERS

2 3 JUL 2018

29/8/18

ALSO BY WILSON HARRIS

Fiction:
Palace of the Peacock
Far Journey of Oudin
The Whole Armour
The Secret Ladder
Heartland
The Eye of the Scarecrow
The Waiting Room
Tumatumari
Ascent to Omai
The Age of the Rainmakers
Black Marsden
Companions of the Day and Night
Da Silva da Silva's Cultivated Wilderness and Genesis of the
  Clowns
The Tree of the Sun
The Angel at the Gate
Carnival
The Infinite Rehearsal
The Four Banks of the River of Space
Resurrection at Sorrow Hill
Jonestown
The Dark Jester
The Mask of the Beggar
The Ghost of Memory

Poetry:
Fetish
Eternity to Season

THE SLEEPERS OF RORAIMA: A CARIB TRILOGY

AND

THE AGE OF THE RAINMAKERS

WILSON HARRIS

INTRODUCTION
MARK A. McWATT

PEEPAL TREE

The Sleepers of Roraima
first published in Great Britain in 1970
The Age of the Rainmakers
first published in 1971
both by Faber and Faber
This new combined edition published in 2014, 2018
Peepal Tree Press Ltd
17 King's Avenue
Leeds LS6 1QS
England

ISBN13: 9781845230975

Supported by
ARTS COUNCIL
ENGLAND

CONTENTS

Mark A. McWatt: Introduction   7

The Sleepers of Roraima

Author's Note   33

Couvade   35

I, Quiyumucon   59

Yurokon   81

The Age of the Rainmakers

The Age of Kaie   105

The Mind of Awakaipu   121

The Laughter of the Wapishanas   139

Arawak Horizon   153

MARK A. McWATT

THE AMERINDIAN FABLES OF WILSON HARRIS

The two collections of Amerindian Fables which Wilson Harris produced in mid-career – and which are here collected in a single volume – can be seen as Harris's attempt to understand and communicate aspects of the history, culture and lived experience of the Amerindians of Guyana. They are not attempts to provide a "factual" or ethnographic accounts of the different peoples these stories reference, indeed, they question the validity of such descriptive, supposedly empirical approaches, sometimes no more than traveller's tales. Whilst Harris is by no means the first Caribbean author to write fiction about the first peoples of the region, earlier novels, such as Edgar Mittelholzer's *Children of Kaywana* (1952) and H.G. De Lisser's *The Arawak Girl* (1958), tended to be historical in approach, attempts to reconstruct a vanished past and often trapped within manifestly colonial stereotypes.[1] Again, there have been other Guyanese writers who, following the valuable 19th century and early 20th century work of ethnographers such as Everard Im Thurn and Walter Roth (the latter referenced by Harris) have been drawn to the narratives of Amerindian myth and legend in both poetry and fiction. A.J. Seymour's "Amalivaca", Michael Gilkes's play *Couvade* (first performed 1972) and Jan Carew's reworkings of Amerindian myth as folk stories for children in *Children of the Sun* (1980) are examples of conscious attempts to locate Amerindian narratives and figures within a Guyanese national literature.[2] Harris's approach in these stories or fables is very different. It is neither

7

conventionally historical or empirically descriptive, but seeks to bring the historical and the contemporary into a complex dialogue that reinterprets these narratives and figures that have come out of the past for their relevance to a cross cultural view of a future human community. As such, the stories also represent a very important gateway into understanding this author's fictional concerns and techniques.

If the fables in this collection don't appear to engage directly with the actuality of the social position of Amerindians in Guyana in the late 1960s when the two collections were probably written (they were first published in 1970 and 1971), it is still worth making a brief note on that context, because, as the story "The Age of Kaie" suggests, Harris's work is never as politically disengaged as it might appear. The causes and indeed the events of the Rupununi uprising of 1969, which involved the ambitions of the mainly European cattle ranchers of the savannahs and Venezuelan mischief-making over disputed national borders, undoubtedly also involved the discontents of Amerindian peoples both as victims of alleged state violence, and as actors in the revolt.[3] The uprising located Amerindians on the political stage, connected in part to the fact that the political party many Amerindians supported, the United Front (UF), a white-led, strongly Catholic party, had just been dumped by Forbes Burnham's PNC after the rigged 1968 elections, from the coalition that had brought the PNC to power in 1964. The uprising reminded at least some Guyanese that the first of Guyana's six peoples was in its economic and social position unquestionably the last. Yet the 1960s was also the time when the long population decline and cultural impoverishment (at the hands of at least some of the Christian missionary interventions) began to reverse, when Amerindians began to look for some political role and the leaderships of the dominant African and Indian political parties began to see the Amerindians as a group that might be worth co-opting and their culture acknowledged as a national ornament.[4] If in *Palace of the Peacock* (1960), Harris was able to locate the "Arawak woman" with her "stillness and surrender" and "reflective pose" as somehow outside the competitive identities of his quarrelling crew, the events of the Rupununi uprising made that image harder to

8

hold on to, and if the stories in this collection don't reference the generally difficult relationships between Amerindians and other Guyanese, they certainly explore conflicting identities between different Amerindian communities. (Since the time of the writing of *The Sleepers of Roraima* and *The Age of the Rainmakers*, it is worth pointing out that Guyana's first peoples have been organising and speaking for themselves in much more extensive ways.)

One can see behind the fables in this collection an impulse that was much more profound than the attempts to co-opt politically and ornament the state. What Harris may be seen to be doing is questioning how the Amerindian legacy might offer some vision of human community that surpasses the prisons of race and ethnicity that have trapped Guyana in division and underdevelopment for the past sixty years. To embark upon this project Harris had to work with such slender scraps of information as existed – mostly in the form of tribal lore and reputation that has been passed on down the ages.[5] Harris speaks of himself as:

> the kind of writer who sets out again and again across a certain territory of primordial but broken recollection in search of a community whose existence he begins to discern within capacities of unique fiction.[6]

He emphasizes the "uniqueness" or originality of the fiction that results from this kind of process by attempting over and again to distinguish it from traditional notions of fiction. He speaks of a "fiction of implosion", of elements of "dialogue or dialectic" rather than "persuasion"; of "fulfilment", rather than "consolidation".[7] All these distinctions imply that Harris is conscious of working against the mainstream of fictional techniques and values, against a tendency to conscript his material – his original vision – into comfortable, known paradigms and models. He is therefore very much concerned with the problem of form – how is the original vision to be shaped, contained and communicated.

In connection with this, perhaps Harris's most important distinction is between what he calls the "novel of persuasion" and the "drama of consciousness". By now these phrases have become clichés in the discussion of Harris's writing, but they do highlight the essential quality of his own writing in distinction to other types of fiction. He explains that in the drama of consciousness, the "writer is involved both as a passive and a creative agent."[8] This dual capacity or function – "passive/creative" – can be seen to apply to the notion of form as well. Northrop Frye tells us we can think of form in two ways "as a shaping principle or as a containing one."[9] For Harris's fiction both of these ways seem to be simultaneously applicable: the form shapes as well as contains the "drama of consciousness", and therefore appears to enter a conspiracy of paradox: to involve the duality and opposition that is typical of all aspects of Harris's writing. Form becomes problematic, dense and convoluted, in order to express a vision of originality, rather than simply to persuade the reader of an inevitable or comfortably familiar social and moral order. The passive/creative paradox thus comes to apply to the reader himself as he is forced to help create or recreate the form and meaning of much of Harris's fiction.

In these seven "fables" Harris is exploring the "void" of Amerindian culture and history. He has complained about "the documentary stasis of Amerindian culture"[10] and he warns:

> It is possible to consolidate the usual picture of the Amerindian, and by clever narrative construction gain apparent clarity or coherency, sensational chronicle or even sensitive documentary. Nevertheless the poverty of conception in such enterprise remains enormous. Indeed if history has anything to tell us, it is of the danger which resides in the wilful conscription of primitive character: a uniform consolidation of so-called historical features through an account of deeds whose motivation or mind we have not penetrated leads inevitably to vulgarization or tyranny.[11]

This "vulgarization or tyranny" is avoided through a willingness to "participate imaginatively" in the life of a community often labelled as primitive:

> Such a willingness... borders upon a confession of weakness, and this, therefore, paradoxically, supplies the creative wisdom or potential to draw upon strange reserves and perspectives one would otherwise overlook or reject, detached as we feel we are within our absolute tower of strength (false tower of strength.)[12]

What Harris is rejecting is the ethnography of the colonial vision, which arrogantly asserts its capacity to pin down and understand the cultures of colonised peoples – particularly so-called primitive ones – from the unquestioned perspective of Western "scientific" rationalism, the "false tower of strength". Instead, the latter course of "imaginative participation" is the one chosen by Harris in the fables and it obviously has implications for the form of these tales. Harris himself uses the term "fable" – and here he means fable in the sense of a story not based on fact; yet, paradoxically, the stories in some sense replace, or substitute for, factual history and cultural data. Harris is seeking to retrieve, through a process involving the capacity for originality in the creative imagination, the vanished truths concerning the tribal remnants that are the subjects of his investigation.

★ ★ ★

The first three stories, originally published as *The Sleepers of Roraima*[13], were subtitled "A Carib Trilogy", and they represent Harris's imaginative investigation into the consciousness or mind of the Carib people, of whom in the contemporary Caribbean only a few remnants remain.[14] As his prefatory note to each story indicates, there is not much to work with; the little known vestiges of Carib myth or history Harris probably found in such sources as W.E. Roth's *Enquiry into the Animism and Folklore of the Guyana Indians* and the translation, also by Roth, of the writings of the nineteenth century German explorer Schomburgk.[15] But these fragments of Carib myth or lore are seen by Harris as areas of entry into the lost mind or motivation of the Carib people. He does not use them "to consolidate the usual picture"[16] of the Caribs, but rather to explore, explain and in some cases even subvert that "usual picture".

The prominent received features of the Caribs are an historical reputation as fierce conquerors, as the cannibals of Colonial Spanish justification for Christian conquest, and now as an extinct or vanished race – the crude essentialism of the racialised discourse that states that "the only 'real Caribs' are the 'pure Caribs'… and the only 'pure Caribs' today are 'dead Caribs".[17] Harris could have made his stories conform to these widely accepted generalizations and therefore embody such values as clarity, coherency and consistency, but instead he chose his own stated methodology of investigation, which "borders upon a confession of weakness" and therefore enables him to "draw upon strange reserves and perspectives" in order to enter the Carib mind that lay behind their presumed or recorded deeds. This point is a very important one for understanding the crucial creative imperatives that resulted in the matter and form of these fables. Again it has to do with the notion of originality, with a primordial quest for source, and the source of human acts (including such large "acts" as civilization, culture and history) in the human mind or imagination. In other words, for Harris, as a philosophical idealist, understanding does not come from studying empirical facts about human culture, but from exploring the architecture of the mind, because the mind is the source of human culture.

The truth of the perceiving mind, the subjective consciousness, is presupposed in the features, of the object of perception/reflection. Thus, through Harris's processes of imaginative exploration, mind encounters mind through the mediation of the object or fragment – and this is the non-material, non-spatial arch of community that he speaks of in the "Rainmaker's epitaph"[18]. So that the imaginative writer reflecting on Carib vestiges takes as his object not any one of the dissonant residual grains of Carib legend or ritual, but rather the truth of the subjective imagination which is travelling that spaceless, timeless arch of community in quest of the important constitutive dimensions of the mind or imagination which is responsible for the act and the vestige.

We find, when we read the three Carib fables, that their form is made to reflect these preoccupations with exploration and encounter. Each circular exploration of the myth or fragment gives birth to deeper and still deeper circles as the author's imagination probes for the mental landscape of the tribe; hence the stories tend to have circular patterns. In the first story, "Couvade", for example – where Harris is investigating the origins of Carib belief and identity through a ritual dream of a constitutive history – the circular patterns are evident. Simply in

12

physical terms Chapter Three is the longest section of the story and the one in which the weave of pattern and event is closest; this is surrounded by two shorter, and then two yet shorter chapters or sections. There is therefore the suggestion of three concentric circles, each deeper and more "difficult" as you move towards the centre. For the reader this suggests either the whirlpool or vortex which sucks him in, or the downward and then upward helical movement that can be seen in the linear progression of the story (like a diameter reaching across all three circles and connecting them).

There are other inward-tending concentric circles in the story: Couvade is surrounded by a blanket (and his dream sometimes described as woven thereon) and again surrounded by the circle (or re-entered womb) of the cave of ancestors, in which is somehow contained the "great circle" of the journey of Couvade and his grandfather. Also in terms of literary patterns there is a circular "Exodus" movement, which is in turn circumscribed by the heroic cycle – from birth, through the death or disappearance of the hero, to his triumphant re-emergence – and this movement is itself in turn framed by the dream. We note as well that the two above mentioned patterns conform with each other – the Exodus movement is contained entirely within the central chapter (Three), the two flanking sections (Two and Four) are concerned with the descent and re-emergence with respect to the underworld of the hero and the same symbolism of river and bridge dominates both sections. There is also an insistence upon patterns of three (three disguises/three ruses) and upon the perception of "nothing" that occurs in both sections. Chapters One and Five complete the largest circle of the dream, from which Couvade probably does not awaken.

The story seems to be closed and ironic, the closed circles suggesting the closed and extinct race of the Caribs. Other features of the story also imaginatively illuminate aspects of Carib reputation. The confusion, for example, between friend and enemy, "huntsmen" and "fishermen" of night – self and other – is a comment on the Carib practice of not taking their women with them on their journeys of conquest, but taking wives from the tribes they conquered; hence there was always a confusion of identity within the community, the women spoke a different language from the men and the child (Couvade) embodies both self and enemy, as the story ultimately suggests. It also manages to suggest that the logic of this practice leads inevitably to an eclipse of the "original" Carib identity. They were the fiercest warrior tribe who conquered all enemies, but in the end were ironically exterminated by their own domestic arrangements, so that their enemy tribes flourish all over the landscape while they survive only in a few remnants. The name "Couvade" itself seems to reinforce this irony: the story ends with a repetition of the information that the name means "sleeper of the tribe", and this suggests that the life of conquest ends in an obliterating sleep, the erasure of waking consciousness and of the knowledge and certainty of identity.

This sense of paradox is embodied in the stories' form – in complexity and circularity – as well as in the notion of the dream from which the dreamer never wakens. In "Couvade" we find suggestions of a number of different forms superimposed upon each other. There is the containing dream-vision and the various Biblical forms and movements which suggest correspondences or links between cultures and peoples. These also suggest that such forms are native, not to particular tribes, but to the shaping capacities of the imagination itself; that these are the forms into which the imagination organizes the mysteries of human existence. The echoes of the Genesis story in "Couvade" – complete with the forbidden food and the banishment for disobedience – enrich form and content by intensifying the notion of the immaterial, mysterious *web* of the arch of community; at the level of mind and imagination, mystic forms and contexts cohere as the features of an original act or *conspiracy* of community.

A further point that can be made about the form of "Couvade" and of the other tales is that their complexity functionally echoes and reinforces the complexity of the process of investigation. The complex form deliberately subverts any expectations of ease or comfort in that process, for such expectations lead, as Harris points out, to "vulgarization or tyranny";[19] to the complacent consolidation of ruling prejudice concerning Amerindian peoples, rather than an authentic encounter, however terrifying, with the *mind* that produced their act of community.

In the second story, "I, Quiyumucon", Harris is investigating the Carib notion of a first cause or ancestral time; by also referring to a "causeway" or bridge he seems to be highlighting the period of great Carib voyages of conquest whereby they "bridged" formidable seas and spaces, but ironically arrived at the mechanism of their own extinction by leaving their womenfolk behind and taking wives from their conquered enemies.

Again in this story we find that the dream vision is a dominant formal ploy whereby the modern mind, in the person of the researcher/narrator who becomes Quiyumucon in his dream, enters the vanished life of the tribe. Here the central ritual of identity is not a dream of genesis nor confused identity, as in "Couvade", but the ritual murder by Quiyumucon of the warrior Queen, his bride, the only fit companion for the Carib man. It has overtones of several other such rituals of sacrifice, including the biblical example of Abraham and Isaac and the sacrificial crucifixion of Christ. It is performed to procure a positive attribute or value:

> …Therefore to make a sacrifice of her was to begin to harden our heart – the pooled heart of the tribe – against all who followed – foreign brides, foreign mistresses, since having slain what was closest and best we knew that none […] could deceive us and draw us from the path our duty."[20]

The harsh determination here is reminiscent of the ritual sacrifices in some central American civilizations in order to re-create the sun, the giver of life.

Harris seems to be attempting to enter the spirit of all such sacrifice in order to understand its essential meaning rather than simply repeat its external (shocking) features when viewed from an alien perspective. While the sacrifice of a loved relative for the sake of the anxieties and self-image of the larger community is a frequent theme of literature, it is far less easy to understand from inside the philosophical and moral enigmas involved. To take one literary example: we find that Okonkwo's sacrificial slaying of Ikemefua in Achebe's novel *Things fall Apart* represents values and motivations that are roughly equivalent to those on the surface of Quiyumucon's sacrificial murder of his bride, but in the end this incident in Achebe's novel is another bit of external evidence of the "falling apart" of the community due to excessive admiration for the masculine principle and its stern values. The fictional vessel that contains the incident remains intact, comprehensible, its form and moral context secure. In Harris, there is the difference that he is working backwards from the fact of a vanished race and that the story's form is subjected to what he would call an "implosion" – a bursting inwards – as a result of the sacrificial slaying. The story itself and its moral diagrams, far from neatly unravelling ("falling apart") at this stage, becomes instead more dense and complex because the attempt to purchase stern images of self with the blood of love is both a beginning and an ending. It becomes the first time or moment of Carib history in which the essential features of personality and civilization are contained. Hence, like "Couvade", the story is ironic, for the "beginning of beginnings"[21] as Harris calls it, also contains the seed of self-destruction.

When images of self begin to be established and valued through the discernment of a pattern of sacrifice beyond human compassion or love, then the formal diagrams (the journeyings) in the story become circular and demonic:

> Poli wondered [...] whether it was a kind of commanding death-wish, the death-wish of a primitive people, superstitiously impelled by the race of the dead, the mask of the dead which they must somehow preserve unbroken, even if it meant a voyage to extinction.[22]

The death-wish is in fact expressed in the form of the story with its demonic circles, including the circle of the containing dream, from which the researcher/narrator awakens and returns to the time/perspective wherein the Caribs are a dead or vanished race.

In the story "Yurokon", Harris is concerned with the ways in which the Carib self-image may itself have been subtly undermined by certain longings and superstitions. He sees the myth as an area of imaginative escape to and from the uniform historical portrait of conquest associated with the tribe:

> ...when we look very closely at Carib vestiges I believe one sees that there has been a divergence at a certain moment of time in

> terms of the bush-baby omens that pointed [...] towards a
> subtle annunciation of native host consciousness.[23]

In his essay, "The Amerindian Legacy", Harris writes about bush-baby spectres as "an omen of demise, a warning of imminent collapse, as well as a rebirth..."[24] In keeping with this perception of a subtle change of emphasis (from conqueror to native, from death to rebirth) the story has a protean, metamorphic form or mode, as times, characters and even cultural and religious contexts fade into each other and seem finally to be resolved within the dominant metaphor of music, the symphony that embodies opposition but is essentially a statement of harmony or unity.

In the story we find features of landscape fading into each other, sky becomes sea (Yurokon's kite is transformed into an octopus) as the story touches all the landscapes and landmarks of the Carib journeyings in order to express the idea that they have finally come to rest in Yurokon, the first *native* – as opposed to the fleeting conquerors who swept across the land and vanished into the next horizon of conquest without acknowledging and belonging to features of landscape. Hence in this story I think we find a concentration upon landscape as native to the imagination and vice-versa, a concentration upon the phenomenology of human presence in the world, in which "consciousness" and "world" can be reciprocally related. A human scale of existence requires an essential involvement with landscape and Yurokon, the bush-baby whom Harris equates with the *genius loci* of another tradition, is the first Carib to have perceived and therefore possessed his landscape. His death in the savannah fire is transcended or sublimated through an overlay of Catholic ritual and symbolism, having to do with the celebration of Easter. The flying of the kite (a tradition of Easter Day in Guyana) therefore symbolically suggests a kind of resurrection. Perhaps, therefore, it is possible to discern in the movement of the three stories the form of the Christian cycle of reality – from original sin to sacrifice to redemption.

Thus Harris's concept of Carib history, though it appears bleak and ironic in parts, does include a notion of the transcendence of the distress occasioned by the sense of loss – loss of origin, loss of innocence, loss of life (Yorokon's death in the savannah fire is the virtual extinction of the tribe); and the transcendence of tribal distinctions as we arrive at a perception of the unity and community of all articulated moments of man's presence in the world.

The stories that follow are from the second volume of fables, *The Age of the Rainmakers*[25], and these continue the exploration into unrecorded pasts and the re-creation of original features of mind through the imaginative processes manifested in *The Sleepers of Roraima*. Here Harris is not dealing with the vanished Carib people, rather the protagonists of the four stories are respectively Macusi, Arecuna, Wapisiana and Arawak (peoples who are still present in contemporary Guyana), and Harris is seeking to uncover the paradoxical spaces behind and within monumental deeds and masks of ethnographic reputation.

In these stories, too, there is the familiar use of the imagination as a bridge between the past of the tribe – the scraps of history and lore and the names of prominent tribal heroes – and the present, where, without a written record, the historian or researcher must rely on the tribal tales and rumours as well as the prominent features of landscape which have remained unchanged: the mountains, the forest with its flora and fauna, the rivers, the waterfalls. Thus in the story, "The Age of Kaie", Harris makes use of the Macusi legend of the hero Kaie whose sacrificial journey over the lip of the Kaiteur waterfall – at the behest of the god Makonaima – redeems the tribe at the time of Carib conquest. In Harris's story Kaie is both the heroic ancestor as well as his contemporary descendant. The contemporary dimension of the story hints at the brief Rupununi rebellion of 1969, quickly put down by the army of the newly-independent Guyana, and Kaie is a fighter in the rebellion who is forced to echo the earlier sacrifice of his ancestor in order to escape from his enemies as well as to rout the enemy of drought (he is, after all, one of the tribal rainmakers being celebrated in these four stories), which is just as serious a threat to the livelihood of the tribe. The sacrifice of the ancestor Kaie, going over the waterfall in his canoe, is somehow re-enacted by his present-day namesake and descendant – simultaneously a victim of the government soldiers as well as the successful rainmaker whose sacrificial death ends the drought as the waters rise and the flood sweeps him towards the lip of the waterfall.

"The Mind of Awakaipu" is a perfect example of Harris's point about the necessity for imaginative investigation beyond the uniform prejudices of perception applied to a deed. In this case the impetus for Harris's fable – as indicated in the note at the beginning of the story – is a tale told by Michael Swan in his book *The Marches of Eldorado* (1958)[26]: an Arecuna Indian called Awakaipu is said to have displayed extraordinary stoicism and indifference to pain when he was bitten by perai (the Guyanese name for piranha fish). But the "stoicism" of Awakaipu at which Swan marvels is an imposed, ready-made explanation of his deed, rather than a rigorous investigation of it from within. Harris takes the scrap of story (though he changes the biting creature from perai to a snake) and his own familiarity with the relevant landscape of mountains and gorge – and the snakes and other creatures that inhabit them – and weaves a vision where the writer enters the character and name of the protagonist and begins to sense imaginatively the reality that gave birth to the legendary stoicism. In so doing the author is able to bridge the two worlds – past and present, Amerindian and European – so that, for instance, the snake that bit Awakaipu (in Harris's story) becomes the snake in the garden of Eden – in a vision that "released the fatality of the universe from an unconscious snake upon god's wrist into Awakaipu's tree of Adam". In this way both cultural traditions (Christian/European religion and Arecuna tribal legend) are modified and enriched by the juxtaposing and cross-fertilization upon the bridge or "causeway" that the imagination can create between cultures. Hence the form of the story suggests the seething natural landscape (gorge of Awakaipu) behind the peaceful mask of his stoic countenance.

It is in a similar fashion that Harris confronted, in the three Carib tales, the "shocking act" of cannibalism of which the Caribs, even in their very name, stood accused. By juxtaposing cannibalism with the Catholic sacrament of Eucharist in the story, "Yurokon", he achieved a subtle erasure of the boundaries of prejudice within which we have always tended to see the Carib reputation. There is a kind of revisionary logic to the fables whereby we simultaneously subject to scrutiny the mind of the Amerindian peoples and our own minds with their accretions of privilege and prejudice. Ultimately the two minds meet across the "arch of community" (Rainmaker's Epitaph) and thereby strengthen its all-embracing web.

The tribal remnant or rumour at the heart of the brief tale entitled "The Laughter of the Wapishanas" is simply their reputation as a "laughter-loving" people. As was the case with the "stoicism" of Awakaipu, Harris feels the need to explore imaginatively this reputation for laughter that attaches itself to the Wapishana tribe. The story's protagonist is a young girl who bears the name of the tribe itself (Wapishana) and who sets out to recover the gift of laughter, since the "Elder tree of Laughter" appears to be succumbing to the cruel drought. In the story laughter is associated with rain and plenty, as opposed to drought and hardship, and the story proceeds in terms of the living environmental signposts familiar to the tribe. Wapishana travels from the drought-stricken "Elder Tree of Laughter" to the other successive existential markers of the consciousness of the tribe: "Elder Tree of Bird", "Elder Tree of Fish", "Elder Tree of Animal" and "Elder Tree of God". In this way the story embodies the familiar motif of the journey or quest that was first encountered in "Couvade", the first story in *The Sleepers of Roraima*.

Wapishana's understanding grows as she explores each of these signposts until she is enabled, finally, to have a perception of god: the "Elder Tree of God" is the final signpost and there she discovers again the gift of laughter, which suggests abundance and rain and the end of the drought. But, as with all the stories, the important thing is the journey itself or process towards understanding the self and the world – and thus unravelling the mystery of the tribe or community.

The final story in *The Age of the Rainmakers* has baffled many with its hieroglyphs and numbers and its radical impenetrability of form and meaning. I think one may look upon it simply as completing the logic of the processes we have been examining in this introduction. In "Arawak Horizon", originality and form have become synonymous; each is expressed by the other.

The numbers are hieroglyphs of space described in the story

as springing from the finite realities of landscape, but are nevertheless intimately associated with the infinite flux and possibility of imagination and creativity. This infinity and boundless possibility seems somehow to inform or shape the tale itself. In "Arawak Horizon", the features of the finite world are metaphors of infinity. Harris uses the basic numerals literally to illustrate the ultimate spatial paradox (which is also the passive/active paradox as applied to form) – first, the numbers themselves are enclosures, definitions, ornaments of space, but the imagination, leaping and playing among, them liberates them from the prison of original place and thereby discovers the self-revelation of the creative process. In re-sensing the origin of mathematics, Harris also discovers the mechanism for the liberation of the first prisoner of life; the proliferation of numbers liberates the prisoner from the stasis of self by symbolizing the simultaneous "other" and the infinite, playful possibilities beyond. No doubt Harris was also influenced by the fact that certain Central American civilizations (relations of the Amerindians of his stories) had achieved an enormous mathematical sophistication – including a knowledge of the concept of zero. Hence the original numbers of mathematics would live within the game of origins he is playing in these fables.

★ ★ ★

Thus far we have been concerned with originality in the sense of a new form which might contain the original content of Harris's imaginative visions or revisioning of Amerindian culture. But we have also, perhaps, begun to approach "originality" in its more profound (and indeed etymologically prior) sense of a primal or original reality or datum, rather than simply as referring to the "unique" or the "novel". In this sense there is perhaps an *original* human community of which we retain some sense or suspicion in our visionary or imaginative capacities – hence the resemblances of Harris's genesis myth of the Caribs (in "Couvade") to the Biblical story of Genesis. The features, such as the eating of forbidden food and the consequent punishment, are, for Harris, not simply features of a story or a number of stories, but rather "original" or originating features of the imagination. Originality, in this sense,

21

appears paradoxically opposite to originality in the sense of uniqueness (the story of Couvade would be *un*original in this second sense since it duplicates features of other myths of origin). Or, to put it another way, the uniqueness does not pertain to the individual story or the individual race that produced it, but rather to the entire human race or community.

In this way Harris seems to be arguing for the authenticity of his fables; they may be stories which are not based on external or objective "fact", but they are nevertheless authenticated by the processes of the imagination which, Harris would seem to think, cannot in any important sense produce "falsehood". There seems then to be an implicit game of paradox involved in these fables; a game of truth and untruth wherein the untruth or unreality resolves itself into a higher reality on a different (transcendent) plane. Harris would probably argue that the imagination is not simply the *only* means of probing the Amerindian past (since no records, other than the archaeological exist), but also the *best* means.

Several other West Indian writers (notably George Lamming, V.S. Reid, Kamau Brathwaite and Jean Rhys) have similarly sought to offer a revisioning of colonial versions of history through an imaginative participation in events of the past for which only partial, incomplete or biased documentation exists, but in a way that does not differ fundamentally from the work of other writers of historical fiction: they are trying to fill gaps in – or provide richer and/or more truthful interpretations of – the "factual" historical record.[27] Harris's process is more fundamental and all encompassing in its claims. This creative process seems more complete and more central to Harris's concerns as a novelist than it does with the others. Wilson Harris, in these fables, willingly enters the void of Amerindian history, where he makes the fullest creative use of the rumours, fragments and legendary reputations that exist in order to arrive at an "original" mythology/ history/lore of the Amerindian peoples.

Part of the discernible qualitative difference in Harris's treatment of history comes about, I would suggest, as a result of the particular philosophical context in which Harris seems to be working. In 1965, C.L.R. James gave a lecture to University

Students at St. Augustine, Trinidad, entitled "Wilson Harris, a Philosophical Approach".[28] This lecture has not been paid much attention, it seems to me, by Harris critics, perhaps because of its somewhat schoolmasterish and condescending tone. But James's basic point is important; he draws attention to the philosophical context in which Harris's techniques of fiction might fruitfully be examined. By referring exclusively to Heidegger and Jaspers, James identifies the context as essentially the existentialist movement, but I would prefer, at least for the purpose of understanding the Amerindian fables, to adjust that context somewhat and suggest that Harris imports into his techniques of fiction some of the tools of phenomenological investigation as seen in the writings of Edmund Husserl, in Heidegger's *Being and Time* (Heidegger was, after all, the foremost student of Husserl) and in such works as Merleau-Ponty's *Phenomenology of Perception*.

All this is not to claim that Harris is writing philosophy in the guise of literature, but simply that his fiction and fictional techniques seem to achieve further levels of meaning and are better explained when viewed in the light of this philosophical context; just as the literary writings of Beckett and Sartre, for instance, are similarly enriched by reference to a particular philosophical context. In his critical writings Harris himself mentions a few philosophers in ways that suggest more than a passing acquaintance with their work, and I think it is not insignificant that he entitles his important essay on investigating vestiges of lost cultures "The Phenomenal Legacy".

In the Amerindian fables Harris can be said to take a phenomenological approach to the questions of time and consciousness as they relate to the vestiges of Amerindian history or culture that he mentions in his "notes" to the stories. Perhaps the point can be better made if we look at Harris's concerns and techniques in the fables alongside certain passages from Husserl's *The Phenomenology of Internal Time-Consciousness.*[29]

In looking at the fables we saw that the question of form seemed to be linked to the idea of consciousness – in all the stories we somehow enter the mind of the protagonist in order to perceive his vision of reality. This has to do too with Harris's obvious concern with overcoming the historical moment, with a perception of reality that is valid both "now" and in the vanished past. According to Husserl:

> All forms of perception presuppose an intentional structure of consciousness, and it is in this intentional structure that the primordial link between consciousness and the world is to be sought.[30]

Thus, as Harris seems to be saying, the factual, historical moment is of minor significance, since there exists "within the structure of consciousness" the clue to his imaginative ("original") perception of Carib history. While one would not go so far as to say that the form of the fables imitates the intentional structure of consciousness, there is frequently, nonetheless, a sense (as in "Couvade") of the reader purposefully negotiating a highly structured pattern of associations within the dreaming consciousness of the protagonist and, by extension, of the author (who is, in any case, initially present as a character in some of the stories). This pattern of association itself then becomes the meaning of the experience.

The form of the fables is also concerned with time; certain paradoxes of time – closed circular movements, confusion between beginning and end, past and future – tended to give shape to the stories themselves. It is important therefore to note that:

> Consciousness is qualified by temporal determinants. Temporality provides the form for perception, phantacy, imagination memory and recollection.[31]

In all his works Harris seems to be dealing, in part, with the way in which consciousness is qualified by time; the way in which the imagination functions by retrieving and juxtaposing different moments of lived experience. It is worth noting that Harris probably extends the notions of imagination and consciousness from the individual to the race or community – in his note to "The Mind of Awakaipu" he mentions his own Amerindian antecedents as if to establish his own imaginative credentials.

The question of originality in the sense, already noted, of origin or primal time is also dealt with in Husserl's essay on internal time-consciousness:

> The question of the origin is oriented towards the primitive
> forms of the consciousness of time in which the primitive
> differences of the temporal are constituted intuitively and
> authentically as the originary sources of all certainties relative
> to time.[32]

In a subsequent clarification he states that he is really concerned
here with:

> the primordial material of sensation out of which arises objec-
> tive intuition of space and time in the human individual and
> even in the species.[33]

What is interesting in these passages is that although Husserl is
using the words "primitive" and "intuitively" in their technical,
philosophical senses, these nevertheless have equal or greater
pertinence when considered in their more common senses in the
context and in connection with Harris's techniques. (In that case
"Objective intuition" would become the kind of paradox that
would embody the spirit as well as the techniques of Wilson
Harris in these fables.) Harris's enquiries into "original time"
("Couvade"), "first cause or causeway" ("I Quiyumucon") and
the "first native" ("Yurokon"), point to his obvious concern with
the general question of origin or originality; and his techniques
themselves assert the primacy of consciousness and such notions
as intuition and imagination over and above the factual or that
which is contained in a specific moment.

Here again, the phenomenological approach serves Harris
well, for it allows him to "bracket" time in terms of actual
historical moments, and to explore characters and situations
outside of time:

> If I add "now" to the idea of man, the idea acquires no new
> characteristics thereby; in other words the "now" attributes no
> new characteristic to the idea of man. In perception, when
> something is represented as present, nothing is added to the
> quality, intensity or spacial determinateness thereby.[34]

Hence, by extension, the factual historical moment is not essential to the business of exploring the quality or intensity of
personality and experience. Thus in several of the stories we get
a deliberate sense of temporal disorientation in order to subvert,

I would suggest, the primacy of the historical moment – to arrive at truths and perceptions that are timeless – and to forestall objections about historical accuracy or historical plausibility.

Another objection could be made concerning the validity of the whole enterprise of enquiry into the dead past of Amerindian peoples – especially the Caribs, of whom, according to Harris, only a few remnants remain. Harris himself supplies reasons for his concern, which are also explanations of his techniques, but in terms of the phenomenological enquiry into one's consciousness of time, the past is of great importance:

> The attempt, therefore, to set forth what is past as something not real or not existing is very questionable. A supervenient psychical moment cannot make something non-real or get rid of what presently exists. In fact, the whole sphere of primordial associations is a present and real lived experience. To this sphere belongs the whole series of originary temporal moments produced by means of primordial associations...[35]

I would suggest that it is precisely such a process of "primordial associations" through which Harris arrives at the origins or at the "originality" of the Amerindian communities he is investigating. Within that chain of associations, or perhaps in some cases, initiating it, are features of landscape which, Harris suggests, modern man possesses in common with the vanished tribes; this might explain his note on Roraima in *Sleepers* – a tremendous feature of landscape which serves as a locus of shared perception across the ages or historical moments – an omen of originality, as it were.

The above is an attempt to demonstrate that some of the ideas and methods of phenomenological investigation can fruitfully be seen to underlie some of the fictional techniques in the Amerindian fables of Wilson Harris. I am not claiming a specific influence or indebtedness, on Harris's part by/to any philosophical work or body of work, although it is interesting that Harris's ultimate resolution of the moments of Carib history in the story "Yurokon" is in terms of notes that make up a symphony: "Annunciation of Music", as father Gabriel says at the end. This parallels an essential image/example in Husserl's attempt to

distinguish durations of time and their corresponding perceptions within consciousness, which involves the notion of the
single phase of a note, the note itself with its full temporal
extension, its lingering echoes in the mind and finally the accumulation of notes to form harmony, which only exists after all the
notes here have actually passed into nothingness. This is paradig-
matic of the sort of relationship I see existing between the
concerns and methods of phenomenological investigation and
the fiction of Wilson Harris, where he makes the fullest creative
use of these techniques and concerns in order to arrive at an
"original" mythology/history/lore of the Amerindian peoples.
Underlying the whole enterprise is his vision of the arch of
community that links modern man with the vanished tribes of
the past, as he says in the Rainmaker's epitaph:

> Originality is the fragile, yet indestructible arch of community
> whose web is akin to, but other than space.[36]

Notes

1. See also Brian Rodway's *In Guiana Wilds: A Study of Two
   Women* (Boston: L.C. Page, 1899); Christopher Nicole's
   Shadows in the Jungle (London: Jarrolds, 1961) and Kenneth
   Ramchand's chapter "Aborigines" in *The West Indian Novel
   and Its Background* (London: Faber, 1970), pp. 164-174.
2. See also "The Legend of Kaieteur", both in A.J. Seymour,
   Selected Poems (Georgetown: author, 1965); Michael Gilkes,
   Couvade was reprinted in Caribbean Classics series with an
   introduction by Wilson Harris (Leeds: Peepal Tree Press,
   2014); some of Jan Carew's Amerindian stories are reprinted
   in *The Sisters and Manco's Stories* (London: McMillan Caribbean, 2002).
3. See Andrew Sanders, *The Powerless People* (London: MacMillan
   Caribbean: Warwick University Caribbean Series, 1987), pp.
   201-203.
4. See for instance the building of the Umana Yana in Georgetown in 1972, and the naming of the National History and
   Arts Council's literary magazine as *Kaie*.

5. This includes some of the texts that Harris references in the introductions to the stories such as Walter Roth's scholarly *An Inquiry into the Animism and Folklore of the Guiana Indians* (Washington, USA: Government Printing Office, 1915; first published as *Thirtieth Annual Report of the Bureau of American Ethnology* (Washington: Smithsonian Institute, 1908-9) and Sven Loven, *Origins of the Tainan Culture*, West Indies (Goteborg: Elanders Bokfryckeri Akfiebolag, 1935). Other important accounts include Im Thurn, *Among the Indians of Guiana : being sketches chiefly anthropologic from the Interior of British Guiana* (London : K. Paul, Trench & Co., 1883).

6. Wilson Harris, *Tradition, The Writer and Society* (London: New Beacon, 1967), p. 54 (my emphasis).

7. Words and phrases from Harris's critical essays in *Tradition*.

8. *Tradition*, p. 48.

9. Northrop Frye, *Anatomy of Criticism: Four Essays* (Princeton: Princeton University Press, 1957), p. 83.

10. Wilson Harris, *History, Fable and Myth in the Caribbean and the Guyanas* (Georgetown, National History and Arts Council, 1970), p. 18.

11. From an essay by Harris called "The Phenomenal Legacy" in *Explorations* (Denmark: Dangaroo Press, 1981) p. 45.

12. *Ibid*.

13. Wilson Harris, *The Sleepers of Roraima* (London: Faber, 1970).

14. See *Indigenous Resurgence in the Contemporary Caribbean*, Ed. Maximilian Forte (New York: Peter Lang, 2006), for a contemporary account of how Amerindian groups have been defining their own futures.

15. Richard Schomburgk, *Travels in British Guyana*, Trans. and Ed. Walter E. Roth (Georgetown: Daily Chronicle, 1922).

16. *Explorations*, p. 44.

17. See Ricardo Bharath Hernandez and Maximilian C. Forte, "'In this Place Where I was Chief': History and Ritual in the Maintenancce and Retrieval of Traditions in the Carib Community of Arima, Trinidad", *in Indigenous Resurgence in the Contemporary Caribbean*, p. 113.

18. *The Age of the Rainmakers*, p. 9.

19. *Explorations*, p. 44

20. *Sleepers*, p. 45.
21. *Sleepers*, p. 55.
22. *Sleepers*, pp. 49-50.
23. *History, Fable and Myth*, p. 26
24. "The Amerindian Legacy" in *Selected Essays of Wilson Harris: The Unfinished Genesis of the Imagination*, Ed. A. Bundy (London: Routledge, 1999), p. 169.
25. Wilson Harris, *The Age of the Rainmakers* (London: Faber, 1971).
26. Michael Swan, *The Marches of Eldorado* (London: Cape, 1958).
27. See, for instance, George Lamming's *Natives of My Person* (London: Longman, 1972), V.S. Reid's *New Day* (New York: Knopf, 1949) and Jean Rhys' *Wide Sargasso Sea* (London: Deutch, 1966).
28. C.L.R. James, *Wilson Harris – A Philosophical Approach*, ed. E.D. Ramesar (Trinidad, Extra-Mural Dept., U.W.I.)
29. Edmund Husserl, *The Phenomenology of Internal Time-Consciousness*, trans. James S. Churchill (Indiana: Indiana University Press, 1964).
30. Husserl, p. 12
31. Husserl, pp. 12-13.
32. Husserl, p. 28.
33. *Ibid.*
34. Husserl, p. 34.
35. Husserl, p. 39.
36. *Rainmakers*, p. 9.

THE SLEEPERS OF RORAIMA

A CARIB TRILOGY

for Margaret
Alexis and Denise

AUTHOR'S NOTE

Roraima (setting of Conan Doyle's *Lost World*) is said to possess the highest mural rock face in the world. It looks towards Brazil, Guiana and Venezuela and one of its Carib names is the "Night Mountain" since it is often enveloped in a blanket of cloud.

COUVADE

NOTE

The Caribs have virtually disappeared as a people though their name is attached to the islands of the Caribbean sea and remnants of their mythology can be traced deep into the South American continent.

This story is an invention based on one of their little-known myths – the myth of couvade.

The purpose of couvade *was to hand on the legacy of the tribe – courage and fasting – to every newborn child. All ancestors were involved in this dream – animal as well as human, bird as well as fish. The dust of every thing, cassava bread (the Caribs' staple diet), the paint of war, the cave of memories, were turned into a fable of history – the dream of* couvade.

COUVADE

1

"The name you bear," the old Carib said to Couvade his grandson, "means *sleeper of the tribe*."

"Why did you give me this name?" Couvade asked.

"Because of your parents…"

"But I do not know my parents."

"Ah," the old man sighed.

"And anyhow what have they got to do with my name?"

"They broke a certain rule." His grandfather's face wrinkled and darkened like a reflection in the river at their doorstep.

"I don't understand. What rule did they break?"

"An old rule. Few abide by it now. We are a dying tribe. A shadow of what we once were." He looked shaken and tired.

"Tell me, grandfather," Couvade insisted. "I'm old enough to be told. After all I am ten years now." His eyes grew a little defiant since he knew there was no record of the day he was born, the month or year, except by word of mouth.

Couvade's hair was black as the river. Thick on his head and glistening in the candlelight of the hut. The old man stroked it gently. In the half-shadow above his grandson's glistening head it was as if he were intent on immersing himself in a river of reflection which ran through him into this uncertain child of the future. He shivered a little thinking how reduced in numbers his people were. They had been almost wiped out over the centuries through foreign invasion as well as inter-tribal conflict. He shivered again. It was cold at night this time of the year. Starred sky. Thick dew. Inky forest.

"Tell me," Couvade said again.

"You were born on a night like this," his grandfather began. "Your mother and father fell sick…" He stopped.

"Please go on, grandfather," Couvade urged. "I do so want to know the secret of my name."

The old man looked away from the boy into the far distance and spoke as if to himself. "They fell sick – it was the sickness of the soul."

"I do not understand…"

His grandfather looked back at him speaking in a strange quiet voice. "It is a dream. A dream of hunter and hunted. You will find it recorded – this dream – on the rocks and in the caves. Hunter and hunted."

"What did they dream?"

"They dreamed – they dreamed the forest grew black as a cave and the stars were extinguished. All they could hear was the sound of wings multiplied like the thunder of a waterfall."

He stopped. But Couvade continued to listen to the ancestral voices of waterfall and forest. He knew of the guacharo bird – how its uncanny reflexes (piercing vision and echoing wings) guided it through the darkest underground caves. It lived deep in the earth where there wasn't a sprinkle of light. Never flew abroad until dark. Carried a star under its wings which the Indians called the "night's eye" and from which they made their candles – large waxlike bait on a hook suspended from the roof.

Grandfather and grandson now sat – two of the last surviving members of the fishermen of night (as their ancient tribe was called) – under the flickering bait of the candlelight in the room.

"I want to know more of my parents," Couvade cried. "Where did they go? What happened to them?"

The old man sighed again. "When you were born and your parents fell ill," he said, "there was only one remedy for their kind of sickness – the ancient remedy of *couvade*. This meant seclusion – a season of fasting and seclusion. They had to shut themselves away from the outside world. No speech with the tribe who would undertake to provide them with vegetables or fruit by leaving it, at the end of each day, at the door of their hut which stood at the end of the village. *No meat or fish.* This was strictly forbidden."

"But they ate…?" Couvade asked with a sudden sense of foreboding.

The old man appeared very tired as if the sap of life within him were declining. He touched his grandson like one who wished to gain strength from his young limbs and to confer at the same time a trickle of wisdom. "They broke the law of *couvade*," he said at last. "They ate what had been forbidden. That very night we were attacked by the huntsmen of night – the tribe to the west of us – and your parents… they were never seen again."

"They were taken prisoner?" Couvade asked breathlessly.

"I cannot tell what happened," the old man said sadly, "I only know they broke the dream of *couvade*." His voice trembled. "It was I who found you, an infant six weeks old, at the entrance of a cave just outside the village where they hid you from the wild huntsmen. I believe they fled into the forest." He shook his head. "I do not know. Perhaps they were indeed taken prisoner."

His voice died away in a dry whisper and the old man and the boy sat, each wrapped in his own blanket of memory and questioning. All was still save for the cry of a bird in the forest asking over and over in plaintive tones, "Who you? Who you?"

2

Later, asleep in his hammock, Couvade dreamt that he had returned to the cave where his parents had hidden him in the nightmare flight from the huntsmen of night. It was as if in his dream he was beginning to understand something of the secret of his name – that he was part of some strange dream of history in which his grandfather's people feared they would vanish from the face of the earth.

The walls of the cave were painted with many curious creatures. Birds. Fish. Men and women who were half-bird, half-fish. Scenes of the hunt. There were two figures in particular that fascinated him and they seemed to be coming alive on the wall of the cave. A man and a woman dressed as curious birds. Perhaps some strange owl or guacharo bird since they wore sunglasses – American sunglasses (in the ridiculous way of dreams) Couvade had seen fall from the sky in the wake of a passing aeroplane. Though they were actually coming alive on the wall of the cave and Couvade felt that all he had to do was reach out and touch them, he had the sensation that they were still far removed from him. Divided from him by water, light, and by other elements. By war: news had trickled through to the last members of the tribe that the great world beyond the great forest, beyond the Carib sea, was at war. It had all happened within the ten years since he was born.

First of all there was water and Couvade decided to swim across to them – the figures coming alive on the wall of ancestors. He would change himself into a fish like one of the paintings there. Half-boy, half-fish. On the other hand if he changed into a bird – half-boy, half-bird – he could fly across the river and approach the two birdlike figures – listen to their conversation. They would accept him as something or some-one they need not worry about, not realizing, of course, that he was a spy. So – in his dream – he made up his mind. There was a feathered head-dress on the ground which he placed over his hair and wings which he stuck to his sides. A pair of sunglasses also which gave him the sense of belonging to the twentieth century while giving him a secretive look as well – an entombed piercing look as if he came from the remote past.

Now that he was ready he began to fly across the dividing river of the cave towards the strangers on the wall. But he felt himself beaten back by a wind of fear. He decided he would never make it in this way and his best plan would be to do what he had first thought of – turn himself into a fish and swim. So Couvade undressed again, took off his glasses, feathered head-dress and wings and clad himself now in fish's scales and eyes.

He slipped into the water and began to swim towards the masked strangers on the wall. He had reached about halfway when he was beaten back again by the water of fear. And in his dream this fear was very strong.

He so much wanted to reach the live figures on the other side of the river of the cave who seemed to him strangers painted there and yet at the same time familiars of flesh and blood. *His flesh and blood. Could they truly be his lost parents after all?* He had now tried wearing two disguises – half-bird, half-fish – in order to reach them but nothing had worked. Nothing had taken him *there.* He had wanted to deceive them so that they wouldn't think him an intruder in their midst... He began to wonder – was it necessary to creep up on them unawares and try to deceive them, if they were really his parents?

Perhaps this was where he had made his mistake. He must go across to them just as he was. No disguises, no tricks.

He carefully restored the headdress, spectacles, feathers to the ground of the cave, the scales and eyes of the fish to the wall where they shone now like stars and constellations. He approached the river to let himself in again but as he was about to do so he was startled by his own reflection. There were faint ripples in the stream which suddenly seemed to give him an entirely wrinkled old expression. He shrank away from the water as if he had been beaten back this time by the *wrinkles* of fear. It was foolish but there it was.

He began to have a glimmering understanding of what was happening to him. In his sleep he had entered the cave of ancestors and was learning to see himself with the eyes of night. The cave of ancestors where nothing was new under the sun and yet where everything was masked and strange.

The cave was very old – old as the womb – old as the guacharo bird: it was very young – young as space – young as an aeroplane whose sunglasses falling from the sky belonged to his own masked parents. Masked curious birds. *They were searching for him, Couvade felt, as he was searching for them.* Lost tribes. Lost parents. Lost child.

Couvade decided that he must look for a bridge to cross to them. Perhaps if he coated himself, powdered himself with earth, his parents on the other side would recognize him as someone who had travelled great distances to meet them and so naturally was as travel-stained as they. They might take pity on him if they saw him in such a guise. So he began to scrape the floor of the cave until he accumulated a small heap of dust, white as cassava bread. This he sprinkled carefully on his brow and hair, arms and legs until he felt he looked travel-stained and weary.

He returned to the river in the middle of the cave and this time he could see himself in the wrinkled water like a branch, all covered with ragged blossom. So ragged that when he shook himself lightly the long accumulated dust of the cave began to descend towards the river like mist. A faint bridge – misty, dusty – stretched now across the river of souls and Couvade set out towards his parents on the opposite side of the cave. He was halfway across when the mist grew so thick he could barely see the back of his hand. He turned and looked back. NOTHING. He turned and looked forward. NOTHING. Yet the bridge stood solid – ages and ages on either side. A bridge which was so travel-stained it might have been formed by the mists of time. Pursuers and pursued. Hunter and hunted. Couvade was uncertain now which end of the bridge he had started from.

He proceeded very slowly and with great caution toward where he judged his parents to be. At long last the mist began to clear a little and he came upon the other bank of the stream. *Yes* – he felt convinced now he had succeeded in crossing the bridge of souls. But – to his sadness – the two parent figures were no longer there. Instead a great forest reached down to the edge of the water: greenheart trees looking faintly silvery and golden. He remembered his grandfather had spoken of this land on the other side of the cave: the forest of the huntsmen of night. No one was there to greet him but he saw that they had left their sunglasses suspended from a branch. Their headdress too and the scales and eyes of a fish like a starry cloak which shone in the water against the trees. Couvade was glad. It was as if they wished to surrender to him all their disguises as he had surrendered his to them on his side of the cave.

The trail into the forest followed the river and he set out along this. He had walked about a hundred yards when he came upon a hill of dust: hill of cassava bread: it resembled the one he had scraped together on the floor of the cave to sprinkle himself with and build his bridge. He poked at it with a finger and a wrinkled face peered out at the heart of the hill, which reminded him of his own reflection in the river not long ago save that this face did not beat him back with a look of fear. It was friendly – an ancient grinning lizard. It changed its colours as it moved – sometimes pale, sometimes dark, sometimes silver, sometimes gold like the hill on which it moved. Silver cassava bread, golden cassava bread.

"You're travel-stained," Couvade said, "like my bridge of souls. I can see that."

"Travel-stained as the rainbow," the lizard smiled.

"I'm looking for my parents," Couvade said.

"I'll see what I can do," the lizard said. "Follow me."

So, still in his dream, Couvade followed the lizard as it moved along the wall of the forest. It kept changing colours all the way – sometimes it looked like a star or a fish, sometimes like a feather or a leaf. It was as if the colours it created were a bridge – an endless bridge spanning all the tribes, all the masks of ancestors. Couvade smiled at the lizard. As he smiled he seemed to wake… Broad daylight… The wizened face of his grandfather stood above him and the wizened hands of his grandfather were shaking his hammock.

3

Couvade had dreamt that he awoke but in truth the wizened face and wizened hands were all still part and parcel of a dream painted on the wall of ancestors. It was so real, however, that it was all coming alive. The tiny village where they lived – painted on the wall of Couvade's dream – stood on its last legs in broad daylight in the night of history. Couvade and his grandfather were amongst the last surviving members of an old Carib tribe who prolonged an ancient feud with the huntsmen of night. The old man said to Couvade in the dream – "Wake up. Wake up Couvade. It's time to move on. Our enemies are after us."

Couvade sprang up and they began to pack their few belongings. First of all the sunglasses which had descended one

45

day from the sky over the jungle in the wake of a passing aeroplane. Next – the headdress of feathers, a relic of the past belonging to the old man's vanished son (Couvade's father). Then – scales and eyes of a fish – a kind of dancer's cloak – belonging to the vanished woman his mother.

"Why must we leave this place Grandfather?" Couvade asked.

"I fear our enemies," the old man said. "They were seen by the cave beyond our village during the night. Skulking against the wall. Those bird-people are no parents of yours. No relatives of any kind. Looking like animated skeletons. Nothing but a trick to take us in – believe me Couvade. We must hide. Conceal ourselves." He pointed to a lizard on the roof. "See," he said. "It has acquired the colour of a dry leaf. It looks like dust. We too must fly like dust in the wind. It is the only way. We must fly – I tell you."

And so they set out – grandfather and grandson and the nightmare relic of the ancient tribe – across the bridge of deceptions – the bridge of dreams painted on the wall of their cave.

They arrived first at the Bush known as the Bush of the Toucan. It stood on the bank of the river and the old man placed the feathered dress that had once been his son's upon Couvade's head. He sprinkled it with dust and said – "This was where my son (your father) stood at the Battle of the Toucan. In those days our enemies were the fishermen of night."

"But… but…" Couvade could not help stammering a little "that is impossible… we are the fishermen of night and our enemies the huntsmen of night… Perhaps you are so old Grandfather that you forget our real name."

"We called ourselves feathers of the toucan long long ago," the old man said, "before we became fishermen of night and our enemies (the fishermen of night) became huntsmen of night."

He again sprinkled – with a cunning smile – the dust of the Place of the Toucan upon his grandson's head. It was like a curious initiation into the secret of names and Couvade recalled the river of reflection and the hill of dust, gold and silver masks of the lizard. It was now daylight in his dream but under the trees against the river, in the very heart of the forest, he felt he stood still upon the travel-stained bridge of the tribes wondering which way to go: dusty feathers of the toucan, misty fishermen of night, black huntsmen of night. They were one and the same – the cruel tricks and divisions of mankind, the cruel ruses and battles of mankind. He remembered the strange birdlike figures he had seen across the river who appeared to be both enemy and friend: he had accepted them as his lost parents, but his grandfather had seen them as animated skeletons, the clever and treacherous disguises the enemy wore – huntsmen of night. He (Couvade) had tried to fly *to* them, swim to them, cross to them, travel-stain himself, dress and undress himself to meet them, whereas his grandfather wished to fly *from* them, run from them, hide from them – hide *in* them (as a last resort) in their cloak, in their name.

"Time to go," said the old man looking back over his shoulder as if he feared his pursuers and looking forward over his grandson's head as if he saw someone flitting before him in Couvade's dream. Hunter and hunted. Could they be one and the same in the end?

"Time to go," he repeated.

"But why can't we rest here?" said Couvade. "I'm very tired."

"Impossible," said the wrinkled lizard face of his grandfather. "We must change our address. Change our colour. We must move on."

So Couvade was persuaded to take the trail again across the Bridge of Ruses – Bridge of the Trickster – Bridge of Tribes. Deeper and deeper into the forest with the river running at their side – sometimes smooth as an infant's brow, sometimes littered with boulders in a waterfall.

"We still have a little way to go to reach the Place of the Fish. It was there long ago that we changed our name: rubbed ourselves all over with the grease of the candle – bait of light – fishermen of night. No longer did we dance by the sun of the toucan but with the shadow of night…" His grandfather paused.

Couvade sighed. Were he and his grandfather running from and towards the same darkness, the same light, the same dance, the same stillness? All these years and still they ran around in a great circle – feathers of the toucan, candle of the guacharo, fishermen of night, huntsmen of night – always one step away from the centre of peace, the end of war.

They paused for a while on the bank of the river to take stock of the Bridge of Masks painted on the wall of dreams. Couvade climbed on the shoulders of a rock. This provided him with a view along the stream towards the Place of the Toucan. It was all very strange because it seemed to lie behind them but yet seemed equally to lie in the mists ahead. A frail rainbow lay across an ancient battleground of memory. Like feathers of cloud. Peacock flag as well as toucan, parrot as well as macaw. Green and red and blue, yellow and white – shade upon shade, shade within shade. It was so exquisite and beautiful Couvade wondered why they had ever left it and whether one day they would retrace their steps into the light of the sun. Whether, in fact, it lay genuinely behind or before them now – at this end of this bridge or that – the rainbow of mankind.

"It's no use," his grandfather said as if he had read his thoughts. "Whether backwards or forwards we must go on to the Place of the Fish. It's less spectacular than the Toucan. It's where we started from when we became fishermen. It's still our only chance." He looked back over his shoulder with the air of a man frightened of both substance and shadow, past and future.

They set out again towards the Place of the Fish. The trees of the forest sometimes shone with flame. First they came to a red tree – a kind of cedar or glowing purpleheart. On one of its branches a beam of sun dangled like a feather, a tuft of feathers, a bright orchid. Shone with such brilliance Couvade thought of a glory of birds, rainbow of the tribes. It was as if as the small party – the last of the ancient tribe – made its way along the Bridge of Souls, one could perceive the trail of the toucan like a strange lizard, a feathery lizard, that absorbed the dying colours of the sun.

Second they came upon a bright-green snake, the parrot snake. It darted on the path before them like a messenger of the elements. Again it seemed like a chain of feathers born of the sun which had pierced the primeval forest in a glancing path upon the Bridge of Tribes.

"Feathers of the Toucan," said his grandfather. "The ghosts of the past. They will lead us to the Place of the Fish."

The trail, in fact, was marked by these witnesses, the feathers of the sun. After the green snake they came upon a russet branch – a bonfire of leaves – burning blossom. Each leaf or feather shone with transparency like the powder of space. One by one, tuft by tuft, each feather of the toucan danced before them. Led them forward upon the trail towards the Place of the Fish.

They arrived at the Place of the Fish towards nightfall. It was an open clearing near the riverbank and in some ways not unlike their other stopping places. In the setting sun – as the feathers of the toucan vanished – the old man placed the scales and eyes of the fish upon Couvade's head. Initiation into the motherhood of the tribe: origins of the fishermen of night. Couvade's mother had been a dancer of the fish.

Couvade gave a cry of joy and pointed to the wall of the sky. Lit up as if for her (his mother's) dance. He remembered the hill of dust which had been sprinkled on his head and which now gleamed afresh like shooting stars. Stars. The largest and brightest he had ever seen. Surely all he had to do was shake himself lightly – as lightly as before when he built his bridge of souls – so lightly that the dust on his head would scatter into a shining net, the brightest, most shining net in all the world. Fishermen of night. Net of stars.

He shook himself now – the dust of stars – as if he too danced to the music of the river. In fact his feet began to move and spin. Ballet of the fish. Dance of the fish. Song of the river. Net of the river. He said to his grandfather in an ecstasy of happiness, "I have caught her. My mother. She sings and dances in my net, in my heart. Song and dance of the fish painted on the wall of the cave."

But his grandfather cried "Hush! it's a trick to make you sleep, then the enemy will take you away, make you her prisoner. *Their* prisoner. Believe me, Couvade, I tell you truly."

Couvade only laughed merrily as if the laughter of the fish made his heart light as a feather. "But I already sleep," he said. "Have you forgotten Grandfather I am the sleeper of the tribe upon the bridge of dreams? What harm can it do to sleep…?" Couvade laughed gaily at the riddle of the night.

But his grandfather cried "There is sleep and sleep. Sleep of enemy and sleep of friend." He wrenched the net from Couvade's hand telling him it was another trick of the enemy, the cunning enemy.

Couvade gave a loud cry. The net which had been torn from his hands settled into the river of night and sank to the bottom of the painted cave. The song of the fish ceased. The dance of the fish was over. He sat now subdued and silent under the shadow of the cold stars.

The small party huddled together (a group of shadowy figures) not daring to light a fire. They munched cassava – dry cakes which dissolved into powder. As the night advanced the cold stars continued to shine on their lips with the dust of bread and the eyes of silent fish, no longer darting and dancing on their painted wall of dreams. The old man was sad. Sad that he had rebuked Couvade. But he had had no alternative. This was Couvade's initiation into the recurring motherhood of the tribe and the recurring death of the tribe, recurring song of the tribe, recurring silence of the tribe. "Soon we shall cease to be fishermen of night," he said sorrowfully to his grandson, "it is time to go."

But Couvade felt miserable and obstinate. He longed to hold again the shining net and hear the music of the river. "I thought you said it would be safe here Grandfather," he complained, "I am sure that was my mother I saw dancing – coming alive on the wall of the cave – on the bridge of tribes."

"It is never safe on the bridge of tribes," his grandfather told him, "what you saw were skulking enemies, animated skel- etons. Your mother? No, I tell you. It was not she. It's another trick. They want to draw us out, make us dance foolishly, make a spectacle of ourselves."

"Shall we become huntsmen of night?" Couvade asked forlornly. "Shall we shed our skins and take the name of our enemies? Then perhaps we shall have come home at last." He spoke like someone repeating the lines of a sad play, a dream-play of history. He was so tired after their long journey. The figure he had been so sure was his mother had now turned into one of their pursuers and enemies according to his grandfather.

Long before dawn (when the night was still black about them) they set out again. First they came to a tree, or what Couvade thought must be a tree, in which the bird of night had settled. He touched the sleeping bird as if he had eyes in his fingers. He remembered the glowing trail of feathers they followed to the Place of the Fish. Now the feathers were inky, black as the trail of night. At the Place of the Fish he had felt he was in the presence of his mother and now, as he touched the sleeping bird, it seemed to him that he was in the presence of his father. His heart began to beat with excitement but before he could take a firm hold on its wings the bird of night started up and flew ahead of him. Its black feathers were displayed where the toucan's had been. It was the most cunning ruse to follow – the trail of the guacharo – the innermost secret of the lizard.

"My father," Couvade cried. "It is he. I felt him under my hands on the tree of night."

"No," his grandfather warned. "It was nothing. I told you before, I tell you again, it was just the night's change of face. Tricks of the enemy."

As the bird of night flew before them however, his impression of his lost father being found returned to Couvade strongly. He related it to the piercing vision of the bird of darkness: how it flew abroad at night within the cave of dreams and was able to penetrate the darkest places in search of food. As Couvade yearned towards it, it descended suddenly and brushed against his lips with a fall of fruit, cocerite of the forest. Couvade was sure his grandfather was wrong. This was no trick. He had touched it with his fingers a little while ago and now, in return, it touched him gently with its beak and wings. "My father" he breathed, so softly that his grandfather would not hear.

The members of the tribe stopped to consume the cocerite on the ground which the bird had given to them. And the bird too – draped in the darkness – stopped overhead, almost within his grasp Couvade felt. Nothing spectacular like the bridgehead of the toucan, flame of the parrot, exotic head-dress of the sun, yet in its outline of memory it seemed to have settled at last, come home at last (his father in an intimate cloak, ancestral bird-cloak, knowing disguise in the wall of night). Couvade reached out with certainty and held it at last. He felt it respond to his grasp, secret and measureless, both creature and creation. As if his father danced too upon the wings of night – as his mother had danced within the net of night. And the feathers of his cloak were a sign of irrepressible humour and confidence. The gaiety of both his parents seemed in remarkable contrast to the sad fierce caution of his grandfather. And yet in some strange way their combined personalities, father, mother, grandfather, represented a royal strain in the tribe.

"My father," Couvade cried aloud as he held the bird-cloak, "my own father at last." But his grandfather cried in turn, "Your father is also my son. This is no son of mine." He tore the cloak from Couvade's grasp and the bird of night fluttered and flew ahead once more. Couvade gave a great sob: he felt nothing now save the shell of cocerite like a sharp quill in his hand. It pricked him with the black feather of night.

His grandfather said to him gently, "I warned you Couvade. Why won't you trust me?" He reached out and touched his arm and as he did so the dawn began to break. Couvade found that he possessed a misty view of the river, back to the Place of the Fish. In the same way – on his journey to the Place of the Fish – he had looked backwards or forwards to the Place of the Toucan. But whereas he had seen the Place of the Toucan arched by a rainbow, he now saw the Place of the Fish arched by a gigantic feather – a black feather, one of the last lingering feathers of the bird of night, the ancestral cloak of night, the *father* of night. In the pale light of dawn, Couvade saw too a dark trail of feathers which stretched from the Place of the Fish to where they now were in the forest. His attention however was riveted on the gigantic feather arched in the sky, upon which the luminous dawn was beginning to shine. As the light brightened the feather of the toucan (feather of day), feather of the guacharo (feather of night) began to dance over the Place of the Fish, the Place of the Fish which was no other than the Place of the Toucan.

The fish-net of his mother, which was no other than the bird-cloak of his father, whirled and danced in the sky, then settled itself into the bridge of dawn. Couvade felt the presence of both his lost parents crossing and re-crossing the shimmering bridge.

4

Couvade suddenly realized as the light broke in the cave – on the wall of dreams – that they had come around in a great circle. He said to his grandfather – "It's our old village grandfather. Village of the fisherman of night. Our old village. We've returned."

"No," said his grandfather shading his eyes against the rising bridge of the sun. "That village lies to the east of us. Yesterday it was to the west. It's the village of our enemies, the huntsmen of night. We shall hide here – in the mouth of this cave – until night falls. Then we shall enter and attack."

"It looks," said Couvade rubbing his eyes in turn as if he were just awakening from his dream – the dream of history, "it looks like our old village – our own village, the fishermen of night."

"It's the old village of our enemies Couvade. I remember it well. We shall descend on them – take their name, mask, colour. We shall become huntsmen of night. It's our safest hiding place. That's why we've come all this way across the Bridge of Tribes."

"Do you mean this will be the last of the enemy? From now on we shall have no one to fear…?"

"We shall wait until night falls. We shall enter. We shall attack."

"But there's no one there," cried Couvade. "The village is empty."

"Everyone is there," said the old man. "Keep your head down or they will see you. The village is full. Full of eyes and old memories. We shall take them by surprise."

During the day the old man laid his plans. Couvade was to remain within the mouth of the cave wrapped in a blanket – the ancient blanket of ancestors upon which the Bridge of Tribes had been stitched with the thread of the rainbow, the feathers of night, the Place of the Toucan, the Place of the Fish. Numerous other travel-stained threads – the threads of fate. The long endless thread and bridge of dreams upon which they followed the design of the enemy back to their own design and homestead – into their own design and hearth – into the design of parent and friend. For the hiding place of the enemy became their own secret like the secret of a friend. Their own home. Their own nest.

The old man himself – who would lead the attack – clad himself in the armour of the lizard. His companions – the remnant of the tribe whom he would lead – also clad themselves in the cloak of the lizard. In this way it was difficult to tell who was old and who young. This camouflage, in fact, was the major stratagem of attack which the old man had in mind. Three phases he explained to Couvade in the mouth of the cave. Three bridges which were the same painting on the wall of dreams.

First, in the light of the setting sun, when they could be observed by the enemy, they would enter the village across THE BRIDGE OF THE AGED. So called because its withered planks looked like bones and skeletons.

On reaching the middle of the bridge they would pause for a while like icons or statues rather than living men. And gradually the chameleon cloak they wore (the armour of the lizard) would take on the colour of the bridge until they turned to sticks – ancient skeletons and sticks. The enemy would laugh as at an army of old men – beaten before the fight began. Thus they would cross their first bridge unmolested.

On the second bridge into the village the enemy would still perceive them (the old man calculated) by the setting sun. This bridge – coming after THE BRIDGE OF THE AGED – was known as THE BRIDGE OF THE CHILDREN. It resembled Couvade's blanket in its markings. Light as a hammock strung across a stream. So light it seemed the first puff of night would blow it away. The armour of the lizard on reaching THE BRIDGE OF THE CHILDREN would turn into wisps of cloth, wisps of thread, a tattered hammock or flag. The enemy would be consoled by *their* approaching enemy which was surely no enemy at all. Babes in the wood. Half-cradle, half-hearse of history. At one moment they looked decrepit and old, shrunken, almost non-existent, the next they looked threadbare, thin – a contemptible flag of souls.

COUVADE SUDDENLY HAD THE IMPRESSION HE HAD BEEN DREAMING ALL HIS LIFE WITHIN THE CAVE OF ANCESTORS AND THAT DREAM HAD BECOME BOTH THE BRIDGE OF THE AGED AND THE BRIDGE OF THE CHILDREN WOVEN UPON THE BLANKET TUCKED AROUND HIM...

Thus far then the old man felt his plans had been well laid and he would safely outwit the enemy. But the third and last bridge – the most difficult of all – remained to be taken. This was THE BRIDGE OF NAMES he explained to Couvade. Here the enemy must finally be drawn and routed by the most secret ruse of the lizard. For on THE BRIDGE OF NAMES in the pale shadow of the sun – the vanished sun – the armour of the lizard would take on the camouflage of *nothing*...

5

The battle on THE BRIDGE OF NAMES began soon after nightfall. The camouflage of nothing the old man wore as his armour, broke down into the idol of the moon, in whose cloak (his own shadow and reflection) the enemy appeared. Long ghostly armies all clad in the light of the moon – the wrinkled face of the lizard – camouflage of sky. This was followed by the march of the stars in whose cloak – idol and reflection – the enemy came. Arrows of light upon the armour of the lizard. Each idol (camouflage of fear) served to block the road to the village of home. "Huntsmen," the old man cried, "our ancient enemy."

"Fishermen," Couvade thought, "our native village."

At long last the retreat began. Was it retreat of enemy or retreat of friend? The idol of the moon fell from the sky. The idol of the stars began to fade. The long ghostly armies crept across the blanket of tribes, the blanket of Couvade sound asleep in his hammock. And in the mouth of the cave where he dreamt he lay since the night his parents ran from the tribe, he too seemed to be passing into the light of freedom – a new sobering reflection – bridge of relationships.

Bridge of dawn upon which the feather of the day and the feather of night danced: bridge of dawn upon which enemy and friend, hunter and hunted, embraced: bridge of dawn upon which the net of his mother and the cloak of his father whirled in a ballet over the Place of the Toucan, the Place of the Fish. Whirled like a hill of dust – a net of stars – a flock of memories – as he, Couvade, shook himself lightly, danced on tiptoe towards the wall of the cave – the bridge of tribes – the bridge of dawn.

And yet because of his grandfather's warnings and rebukes he was still uncertain. Uncertain that the battle of idols, camouflage and armour, was over. Uncertain of the figures coming alive on the wall of the cave. Uncertain there was not a long hard way to go before the idols and paintings would truly melt, truly live, birth of compassion, birth of love. Uncertain he would not have to go around again in a great circle dress and undress, sprinkle himself with dust, travel-stain himself, play the role of both enemy and friend. Uncertain of the riddle of the night – the riddle of his name.

For with the ascent of the sun it was as if all his uncertainties arose and the bridge of dawn – the dance of the feathers – melted: became the siege of dawn – siege of the bridge of dawn – siege of the tribes, long endless retreat. The lizard suddenly ran (WAS HE FOE OR FRIEND?), ran along the bars of Couvade's hammock. Ran like the law, the law of earth, very wily, very cautious, the warning of the law: ran like love, the love of heaven, very gay, very relaxed, whimsical and open. It was the old wrinkled face of the trickster of the tribe – half-law, half-love – looming above him. Waking him. The wizened arms of the trickster lifted him as if he were a child again, as if his parents had just vanished, leaving him hidden in the mouth of the cave. The wizened arms lifted him – aged camouflaged arms – THE BRIDGE OF THE AGED – all bones and skeletons. Lifted him again upon THE BRIDGE OF THE CHILDREN – threadbare camouflaged arms. Took him sternly and warningly to his breast – namesake camouflage – THE BRIDGE OF NAMES. Then on into the village as if he were once again a prisoner of the tribe from whom his parents had fled. Fled from the stern tribe who claimed him (Couvade) as a huntsman of night, the child hidden by his erring parents before their flight.

His grandfather knew they had broken the law of *couvade*, the law of the fast, eaten meat and fish. He had seen them dance when dancing was forbidden. The Song of the Fish and the Song of the Feather – both forbidden. The Song of the Net and the Song of the Cloak – both forbidden. He had seen them run laughing the Race of the Feathers when racing was forbidden. He had seen all this, following them secretly. He had watched them hide the child in the cave of ancestors and had taken him up in his arms, his own grandson, Couvade.

"You are the last in a long line of huntsmen of night," the old man said. "I shall call you Couvade. You must learn caution. You must learn not to break the law."

"*Fishermen* of night," Couvade said pleadingly. "In the beginning you said we were fishermen of night." He recalled the shining net of his mother and the dark cloak of his father, both of which the old man had wrenched from him.

But the old man said, "I was mistaken. The fishermen of night are now our enemies. They live to the west of us. We must beware of their tricks. We must watch. We must listen." His voice echoed in the cave of ancestors and faded...

AT THAT MOMENT COUVADE GLANCED UP AND THERE, HIGH IN THE ROOF OF THE PAINTED CAVE, THE LIZARD SMILED DOWN AT HIM. ITS EYES LOOKED VERY FRIENDLY AND VERY WISE. IT GAVE ITS HEAD A SLIGHT SHAKE AS MUCH

AS TO SAY, "FISHERMEN OF NIGHT, HUNTSMEN OF NIGHT, PLACE OF THE TOUCAN, PLACE OF THE FISH, EAST, WEST, ENEMIES, FRIENDS". THEN IT FLICKED ITS TAIL LIKE THE FEATHER OF THE TOUCAN AND SPOKE.

"The name you bear," the lizard said to Couvade, "means *sleeper of the tribe*."

And it vanished.

I, QUIYUMUCON

NOTE

By Quiyumucon the Caribs meant First Cause or ancestral time. The stages by which this assumption was reached are not disclosed in the scanty historical or mythological records available to us though these are stamped in places by a luxuriant imagination and sense of poetry.

Poli, son of Quiyumucon, is an invention.

I have attempted to see Quiyumucon through the subjective eyes of the late twentieth century as painted Rock-King or ancestor whose association with his people reflects a tradition of sacrifice steeped in uncertain origins and convulsive landscapes, earthquake and volcano.

The records of the Caribs disclose that they were a proud and fierce people with a terrifying sense of order accompanied by a profound ambivalence – guilt and melancholy. There are many speculations as to the land which they originally possessed, and their departure – which was the first step they were to make towards extinction – remains obscure.

Some say their original homeland was Brazil, others Florida and so on. It is known that they mastered the sea – named after them – across which they sailed in Viking formation. They have also been identified with the legendary battledress of the women of the Amazon.

The introduction of a Carib warrior maiden or Queen in this story, therefore, is mythologically consistent though – according to history – the Caribs did not bring their women with them but married their prisoners, Arawaks and others. As a result two or more languages were spoken in the tribe, one by the rulers or men – another by the ruled or women.

My fable of a First Cause or causeway – blind man's ford – is an imaginative exploration of the deed of conquest in controlling as well as assimilating others.

There is the rudiment of a Carib myth to do with an "egg" of creation which passed from the male to the female and this I have adapted to my own purposes.

I, QUIYUMUCON

1

Poli, the son of Quiyumucon, ruling ancestor or King, was in his thirteenth year. He loved the ceremonial objects around him and sometimes he adorned himself with feathers or wore the cloak of a jaguar or blew through a hollow branch or tumpet until the leaves of the forest rained upon him. And then in his imagination he sailed within the hammock of the rainbow to the sacrificial rocks of Quiyumucon.

It was a curious half-drowsing thought within which to dwell as I watched the painted figures on the wall in the vaguely flickering lantern light which shone in the cave. I had arrived there that day (in the year 1970) in the heart of the Bush with a party of researchers, intent on reconstructing a model of Carib mythology. Now night was falling. The other members of the party had fallen asleep exhausted on the ground. I, too, was exhausted yet I found myself seeking to concentrate on Poli and Quiyumucon and at first with uncertainty then with increasing awareness felt myself transported to another world. Poli was winking one eye at me with rare humour and sadness. There was the tinkling of a bell like the distant ripple of running water.

"The hammock and rainbow in which I sail," Poli said to me with a sudden dark grave look far beyond his years, "are now bridges of sacrifice though once they were – in the very nature of the elements – part of a circle or globe or egg of creation."

As one who slept – now with the living Carib dead I paid the closest attention to him as the hammock of dreams stirred. Poli was, in fact, addressing me as if I were his father and idol, Quiyumucon.

His voice rang suddenly with the spirit of rebuke – "Why

must I sail to the sacrificial rocks? Why is it necessary that I do this? Shall I ever reach there and if I do shall I ever return?"

I did not reply. I felt my lips like Quiyumucon granite, cruel as the law. And yet I felt too the strange tenderness of the sand of blood running from the crevices in the ancient wall of ancestors. Poli was piloting his rainbow hammock, a black mask of hair veiling his eyes and lips which were slits of flame. This character of metamorphosis served to accentuate the mask of his features which at one moment seemed to accept and trust me (as when a little while ago they winked one eye) and at another, as in this instant, seemed to burn with hate.

Tall for his age and slender of limb. If I moved that hair aside, that veil aside, I dreamt, his mother would stand forth like a warrior maiden of old: his mother who had secreted herself at the heart of the male host in their retreat from the land of origins, and it was not until they advanced into an area (lying between Orinoco and the mountains of Guiana) which became their new homeland, that her Amazon disguise was uncovered and from breastplate and hair a woman of pure Carib blood stood forth.

I trembled as I recalled the event as if a bird's egg had fallen from the sky and in place of the sun of creation stood a creature still covered in feathers, half-sinister and lovely as the moon. It was a stroke of genius on her part. She had taken advantage of the chameleon of war – long secretive hair of night and curious hidden breastplate of sun – to insinuate herself into the company without arousing suspicion. In fact she consolidated a ruse, then in its infancy, of shock identification, day that resembled night, night that resembled day, bird that resembled beast, beast that swam like fish, woman who appeared like man, man who appeared like woman, to harass and confuse the enemy in the name of Amazon or Viking.

Poli, therefore, as the son of Quiyumucon and the warrior maiden of old, as the last descendant of pure Carib blood, occupied a supreme position in the Carib heartland. This was made manifest when his mother was killed three months after he was born by an arrow that pierced her hammock and breast as she slept. It was now, as I looked back in time at that sacrificial murder, that I stretched forth my hand with infinite pity to part the mask of hair from Poli's brow (in order to identify him beyond a shadow of doubt as my son, after his long sojourn with the priests) – but he shrank away as if an intuition had entered the very core of his being, an arrow of eclipse shot by the bridegroom of the sun across the hammock of the moon.

2

"You killed her," he said to me. "You killed my mother."

I was struck by a transformation of appearances. The place had darkened and the hand of a priest, sawn off above the wrist and presented now on the arm of a long spear, covered the lantern in the middle of the cave to simulate the shadow of eclipse. In this veiled moment the bell of the stream I had heard when the hammock of dreams first stirred began to pound like a cataract of water. We stood within blind man's ford – the first sacrificial waterfall painted on the wall – and before us loomed the other sacrificial rapids like phantoms of order upon a succession of rocks in the dark of the lantern moon.

Poli cried again – "You killed her." I found myself at first unable to reply with the graven lips of Quiyumucon since the metamorphosis of the cave seemed to possess such deadly frightful beauty and earnestness, it flashed not only with the hand of eclipse but with the arrow and rain of spirit. "Yes," I admitted inwardly, "it is true I killed her."

"You murdered her," Poli's voice rang in my ears together with the bell of the stream. I partly wakened then in protest and before I fell asleep again it dawned on me like a consolation that I was party to a dream of ancestral time, standing upon earth's ford of broken celestial water and sky, and Poli's speech was part of a ritual bond and accusation.

I found myself being apprised of the facts. Since the death of his mother he had been in the care and instruction of the Carib priests and this moment – for which he had been schooled beyond his years – was no stranger in time to him. I realized he had been away so long I scarcely knew him at all though he, like myself, was a chosen instrument of the tribe, clay of the psyche.

"I slew her," I said, "in obedience to the command of the priests. And now, my son, come closer. The light is bad. I need to see you better. Listen to me. *You* are alive, *she* is dead." I put forth my hand to lift the black hair painted on the wall but Poli drew back with horror and misgiving.

"Poli," I said strongly, with a note of pleading in my voice, "listen I say. Try to understand. She was the last maiden of our blood – a warrior maiden at that. She helped to forge and consolidate a tradition: the chameleon of war – breastplate and hair."

"You killed my mother," Poli insisted.

"It was a time," I tried to reason with him, "when the Caribs had begun to take as wives the women of a foreign race – Arawaks and others like that. There was great danger that we would be seduced by the soft ways of those we had overcome: wooed away by them from the stern habit of the law. We had to arm ourselves, I tell you, my son, against the guile of our victims. Can you not see this?"

"All I know is that you murdered her," said Poli and he sobbed.

"Poli, *you are our son – mine and hers*," I cried. "Dry your eyes. Tears belong to the weak. Listen. She was very dear to me. The last Carib maiden I knew. When she was discovered by the host of the tribe none of us at first could believe our eyes. Here was our equal – a warrior maiden – think of that – and as such it was the last marriage I, the King, could consummate with an equal in rank and station – warrior to warrior – like day to day, night to night, before the egg of creation was broken…"

"You slew her with an arrow as she slept. That is all I know."

"As one who was dearest and nearest to me," I urged, taking my stand with Quiyumucon, "the very marrow of my bones," I cried to the hand over the moon, "one who was my day when I chose to be day, my night when I chose to be night, one who therefore knew the unity of the stars, pooled yolk of suns and stars and moons (do you understand?), universal egg, self-eclipse, self-illumination, all one, *all one*, I repeat…" I paused.

Poli opened his lips to speak but I rushed on. "She was the last of a perfect line of women, the finest and bravest we knew. Therefore to make a sacrifice of her was to begin to harden our heart – the pooled heart of the tribe – against all who followed – foreign brides, foreign mistresses, since having slain what was closest and best we knew that none (however crafty, however beguiling, however tender) could deceive us and draw us from the path of duty. Can you not see, my son, what an election her death was?"

"Did you look at her?" asked Poli all of a sudden in a soft strangled ominous voice. "Did you look at her face afterwards father?" He spoke the word *father* with a muffled cry that could have been hate or love. I began to tremble then. It was hard to believe that Quiyumucon granite could tremble but I shook as if a faraway earthquake invested the cave.

I knew I had broken the law. I had not parted her hair and robe and looked on her face and breasts as I had been instructed to do by the priests of the tribe. I cupped my hands over my eyes. "No," I told him, "I could not bear to look on one so tender. She was dead. But let me look at you Poli my son. You are alive." I moved the cup from my eyes and though he shrank still farther away from me and I still could not see through his mask – through his hair which fell now as hers fell then – I felt that he smiled secretly and sadly and triumphantly. And that the hand over the moon grew darker still until I could no longer tell if it was he or the ghost of the warrior maiden, his mother, who stood there on blind man's ford.

3

A further metamorphosis of the cave began as the distant tremor and earthquake subsided. The hand of the priest, sawn off at the wrist and extended on the long arm of a spear, covered a lantern sun this time. It was as if I had moved to another sacrificial rock and whereas the first had been an eclipse of the moon, this was an eclipse of the sun. Not – it seemed to me – that the cave was any lighter. It was still blind man's ford on the cataract of the river and the bell of the waterfall still rang at our feet.

Poli had faded into the darkness of the cave but I, Quiyumucon, and the warrior maiden whom I had slain with an arrow, rose now again like grievous stars and constellations of blind day within the eclipse of the sun. She lay on her rainbow hammock, which had been nailed to the faint bark of a tree, scooped and converted into a royal bed or canoe by the priests.

I recalled how I trembled the night I slew her until the granite of which I was made shook like the sea of the sun. I had disobeyed the priests in refusing to lift the veil from her dead face.

Now – upon the shore of eclipse, sacrificial rock – I had been given a second chance. I thought of Poli whose blood would be on my head like an ocean of remorse, epitaph or sea named after us, if I did not obey.

I strove with all my will – a dew of sweat on my brow – but found myself still riveted to the wall. The clamour of wings rose from cataract and river.

And then a thought suddenly came to me. Why should I need to uncover the face of my deed, of my warrior maiden, when the sea of time was at hand to bear it away through and beyond the mirror of eclipse? No need to tremble before a hammock of grief in the shadow of the sun. For surely if this eclipse were such a rainbow of stars like sunrise – bringing back the unwanted mask of the dead – there must be a hidden sunset into which we could sail like the unsculpted yolk of an egg… starless ubiquity… night?

I recalled the first time we had tried to make our own ritual sunrise and sunset of ancestors within which to embark like shadows of the future. With the dawn of day we used to see a flock of brilliant parrots flying from us towards our ancient homeland far away across the sea. With the coming of night they returned and vanished quickly. We observed them closely and read the scroll of the sky as if it were our own ghostly hand up there in space, deed of eclipse over the race of the sun.

Then it was that I, Quiyumucon, with my heart in my

mouth, sought to construct the first bier of time – ship of doom – beyond the hammock of the rainbow. I shot my arrow into space. It pierced the invisible host on the edge of night and one parrot fell, sudden splendid plumage, outstretched wings, sailing within the boat of the sky.

I recalled how I knew I had failed in my plan – how my bier or ship was wrecked even before it had been properly launched – for on securing him, the dead bird, to masthead or bow, the flock materialized and descended towards us confused and violated and wild. It was the first time for them too that a feathered creature, a royal parrot, had been shot from the sky and stitched to the brow of a man painted to harness time to the shadow of his will. They wanted to know whose omniscient wreck of a fleet it was to which their bright trailing feathers were nailed. As they flew around me in a rainbow-coloured flag, like a sail on the horizon of night, I wondered whether they would pluck my eyes out of Quiyumucon granite to confirm the wreck of darkness on my brow, sacrificial rocks, blind man's ford.

Poli now reappeared from the shadow of the cave into which he had vanished and as he stood before me I felt he carried within him the dawning seeds of his mother's death.

4

Poli's reappearance was indeed curious. I realized now that it was not simply a question of his moving into or out of the shadow of the cave but that against a deepening tide of eclipse, constellations normally obscure in the paint of the sun began to stand out with the brush of night on day.

The dawning seeds of apprehension I now associated with him, in connection with his mother's death, extended from his brow like a string of beads or stars. Beneath each seed or bead of star I could discern the sprouting outline of a war canoe moored to a sacrificial rock on blind man's ford.

There were several such canoes and they all stood on the tide of history that had branched with the Viking Caribs across a sea of islands and up the rivers of a continent. Each had been built like exploratory vessels of doom, experimental cocoons, voyages into the unknown. They all bore the masthead of Quiyumucon: they all resembled the bier of his Queen, the royal parrot which marked his failure since he had been unable to overshoot the mirror of sacrifice.

They bore also – these war canoes of Quiyumucon – a heap of ornaments or substitutions; long feathers of night, long wigs of hair, breastplates of sunrise and sunset: the chameleon of the Amazon through which the fierce climax of war had rolled as though within a marriage to all creatures and things, still leaving, however, that irresolution of horizon Quiyumucon dreaded.

So no wonder another effort was contemplated, Poli realized, another ship of doom he discerned in construction within the shadow of the last sacrificial rock of all on blind man's ford. The outlines were still unclear at this stage but as he looked from it back to Quiyumucon – as he looked around at the stern but listless Caribs – he was filled with foreboding about himself and his race. It was as if a gigantic reaction had begun to set in at the very peak of conquest, a gigantic dissatisfaction or exhaustion and a sense that time was running out – that it was now or never the bier of ultimates must be built, which would relieve them of confronting the face of their deeds, long since accomplished in the name of order and now worthless as clay, the clay of the psyche Poli felt in the mirror of eclipse.

Poli wondered – with the wisdom of the priests far beyond his years – whether it was a kind of commanding death wish, the death wish of a primitive people, superstitiously impelled by the race of the dead, the mask of the dead, which they must somehow preserve unbroken even if it meant a voyage to extinction.

As he looked closely at the new vessel now under construction he realized there was one element of importance he could not ignore. Clearly there was no intention of using the effigy of the Queen, his warrior mother, as before. Poli saw that Quiyumucon, in disobeying the priests, had deprived himself of the efficacy of his beloved muse for the last voyage he contemplated into the unknown. She (or it) had worked like a magic charm in taking them up to the watershed of victory but this voyage – this new voyage on the other side of the hill – down the ball of the sea through the reflection of memory – demanded the blood of youth to resist every constellation, to resist every trick – a new masthead of generations – a new pride and will – a new instinct for unreflecting and unburdened decision at the helm of things.

This time, Poli saw, his father sought to placate the priests – to perform the spirit, if not the letter, of the law, by unveiling the one to be sacrificed before the actual event.

"No," said Poli and this time there was a tremor in his voice. "The priests are very clear about this father. You cannot unmask a deed before it is done."

And yet even as he spoke he had approached the new vessel in the shadow of eclipse as if to declare himself its future masthead. Here, beyond doubt, his judgement was confirmed: this was no ordinary canoe. Its essential framework was a kind of wreck. This was accentuated by the persistent flag of stars – ring of birds – which sailed where the masthead of the Queen had been and which Quiyumucon had failed to submerge on the horizon of night when he sought to sail into the unsculpted yolk of all – into the most hidden sunset of time – beyond every reflection of memory within the shadow of the sun.

It was this sense of the omniscient wreck of a fleet of darkness that drew Poli to stand on the last deck of all like a living prophetic masthead in place of the muse of Quiyumucon, and to look back towards the other vessels – each moored to its sacrificial rock – as to a fleet in reverse, all participating this unfinished ship, this ultimate deck on which he stood, whose beginnings lay far back in an original deed of memory, an original voyage of conception beyond a homeland which it became so necessary to erase that the Caribs had fled and invested their flight with exotic phrases like "ship of doom", "bier of time", anything that would nerve them to an implacable austerity, a living and frightful immediacy purged of reflective consciousness.

I approached the deck on which Poli stood.

"No", said Poli again, like a parrot or oracle drilled by the priests, as I stretched out my hand to lift the hair from his face, "you cannot unmask a deed before it is done."

Ruling ancestor though I was I felt it necessary to explain. "Listen," I said, "you stand where the figure of your mother once stood. I have not told you this before but I was blind to her in her life as I remained to her in her death. When my warriors found her and brought her to me she was wild – painted with feathers – chameleon of war…"

"You made her your bride. You must have seen her then."

"All ceremonial our marriage was, I tell you, more paint and processional. I slept at blind man's ford with a maiden of war. Let me look at you my son." I spoke to him as to an equal.

"I will not," cried Poli.

"Do not hide from me now I say…"

"I do not wish to hide father. But the priests have warned and commanded."

I felt a sudden rage. "Priests. Priests. What do they know of action?"

"They know of the action of love father."

"Superstitious love, nothing more, in this Carib sea and sun. We are haunted by it. And since you speak of action my son – it is action which must purge us of the ignorant reflection of love. *The deed is all.* It is useless to pine and look back into the mirror of eclipse. The night I slew your mother I should have come to a compromise with the gods. I should have arranged to unveil her – not after (in the letter of contemplation as instructed) but immediately before (in the spirit of action as intended) – by creeping up on her unawares, moving softly to her hammock while she still slept in the land of the living, though so drugged by the priests as to appear already dead. I should have parted the hair from her face and the armour from her breasts, stripped her of paint and scanned her entirely, scanned the ignorant nature of love, if such there should be, lying there as the naked embodiment of an age. A moment later I could have killed her within a single stroke, sight and execution, as it were, a single round action – do you follow me?

– wherethrough in abolishing her I would have abolished the necessity to look on my deed, since the deed was all and *nothing* could remain afterwards."

Poli stood like stone with his hand over his face and as I put forth my hand to grasp him now, to *see* him as I slew him, the hand of the priest over the sun moved in unison with mine, the eclipse faded and he vanished in a blind painting of light... I could hear his voice, however, addressing me from the ship of space – or if not space (and this was the strangest thing of all) – from the masthead of the future. It was a terrifying gesture of fulfilment. Had I, in fact, accomplished my own wish – so erased the act from reflection – that he stood there now as the universal deed of light, the unsculpted cross of the sun?

I raised the blind hand now that killed my son and the spear of light pierced me then.

5

The swift spear of dawn had now entered the cave and the warning of the priests Poli had transmitted to Quiyumucon began to make itself clear. It was akin to the shattering blood of the fleet of an age – the almost unbearable thrust of sacrificial fire, rather than a gradual muse and digestion of the face of time.

I was half-awake now but dreaming in blind daylight as if still asleep and as I took my stand with Quiyumucon I observed the wreck of his fleet of darkness as it began to fade back into the growing paint of the sun.

It was a curious reality because in a sense as I observed the passage of his canoes through dazed eclipse into the explosive ruin of light I realized that I, Quiyumucon, had gained my desire but in a manner which contradicted my own shadow when I disobeyed the priests.

This was not the horizon of sunset, hidden sunset I desired, but of sunrise, the blind of dawn within which the stars were extinguished.

The sacrificial play painted on the walls of the cave became a calendar of suns which rose and stretched from the masthead of Poli – backwards from the invisible sunset of the future into the formless sunrise of the past and littoral of home upon which the fading fleet of the Caribs now stood: a curious sale or auction of primitive vessels of guilt which were blending into the sky.

It was the auction of a sea of gold in the present and future whose price of guilt, in the bliss of action, I had not understood as a bonfire of sun... it was the auction of the wreck of our fleet through Poli's masthead, bier of light... it was the auction of the deed of kith and kin and the blind of nails in that deed – the sun of paint on my hand concealing Poli's blood – through which I began to discern faintly the hand of the priest that moved and retreated like a clock of ancestors in unison with mine.

This – the clock of the Caribs known as Quiyumucon or First Cause – was the most curious shadowy commodity for sale on blind man's ford. For in it and around it lay a causeway of relationships which brought into new focus the disparate canvas of the fleet. There was the Viking hand of ancestor time and the Amazon hand of warrior Queen upon a sea of gold.

The sun blazed in the rubbled face of the clock and this eclipse – the boulder of sun upon sun – possessed its own flakes and shadows, as the eclipse of darkness upon darkness embodied its own stars.

Quiyumucon and Poli were dancing and leaping with the warrior maiden around the rock of the sun and in their shadow or flake lay the heart of the chameleon of the tribe, the rocking clock of ancestors capable of reconciling the ship of doom with the splintered bier of light, the materialization of fossils in a mirror of eclipse with the dematerialization of darkness in a mirror of suns.

The clock of the ship indeed was a landslide of memory known as First Cause, the causeway of the blind. And it was this deed of the sky which first set the bell tolling at the heart of the cataract like a grievous living blow administered by Quiyumucon within which the first shadow of time, curtain or waterfall, mourned and justified its existence.

In addition to the tolling bell now ticked the clock of the

rock, pendulum of sky, like a glancing arrow diffused and reflected into the second shadow of time, painted flake or rain of Quiyumucon.

It was a saving reduction of scale to which all things now mourned and danced. The flake of Quiyumucon or First Cause turned to a grain of sand like the shadow of an ant. And this began to pace the numberless hours on the face of nature's clock. Hours that secreted to themselves an infinite reduction of the fantastic march of events through the landslide of the sun.

Although the masthead of Poli had once been the top of a living mountain blasted by the lightning of Quiyumucon and as the deed of the sky ran to the sea, sweeping all in its path, Poli became the receptacle of the forces of the land which streamed through him – except that, in the shock of translation, his was a basket or sieve which retained but a shadow of memory, the shadow of sand as the dance of history.

This it was, this dance of scale, that became the balancing role in which I was now absorbed as though I created it all in the very camouflaged beginning when from original chameleon (known as the mountains of Poli) the Caribs were first expelled. These mountains and valleys had been their controversial place in the paint of the sun; and the sacrificial rocks of Quiyumucon (First Cause or Sky) and Poli (mast of earth) were my recapitulation of that lightning feud and expulsion – ultimate fleet – wreck of darkness – endless beginning of beginnings – first causes within undisclosed movements.

The enemy who returned to fulfil a sacrificial role in driving or launching them forth were distant relatives of Quiyumucon claiming equally to be the first tenants of the land expelled in their turn long long before. They came in such superior numbers now that Quiyumucon and his people were taxed to the utmost to defend themselves. And it was then that they began to practise what was to become their ultimate strategy of offence and defence (enigma of war) – the art of metamorphosis which in addition to employing the paint of feathers or the stripes of animal, the breastplate of day or the long hair of night, knew how to advantage itself within a curious reduction of the scale of events.

The camouflage of the ant was first employed to fantasticate into irrelevance the superior numbers of First Tenant now back on the doorstep. He (Quiyumucon) so secretly deployed his forces he was everywhere and nowhere, everything and nothing and this began to wear the enemy down until they were convinced they were involved in a campaign which dissipated their strength, destroyed their morale, wasted their fibre and ate into their reserves like a familiar disease: diseased projection into no one and nothing.

Quiyumucon succeeded in paralysing the enemy for a while until a sheer cliff of numbers coming up from the rear drove him up the masthead of Poli which he held, extending his command into a certain valley whose starved watercourse and environs at this time of the year were known by various names such as the lap of war, the maiden of war, the ship of war.

Then it was a certain inspiration flashed in his mind – a new reduction of scale – his fleet or ship of oblivion. It was time, he decided, to break free from the mountains, descend the valley into the sea, embark for another land, a foreign land, a foreign conquest. This would entail a new trigger, a new trap, a deed of soul to invest both valley and sea. Where the campaign of the ant appeared before like a reduction of numbers, the ship of scale must adapt all things into its camouflage, a silent sea upon which to sail across the land, a silent fish within which to dive through the land, silent beasts upon which to ride in the land – silent forests within which to move – silent birds through which to fly – charmed concert of stillness through and beyond the earthquake of war, the fire voices of the enemy.

Those fire voices crackled and sang and burned closer night after night, day after day, and Quiyumucon felt himself ringed by a fever of hate. He longed for an end and a new unmoved yet farflung beginning – a climate of conquest and extinction where he needed but the shadow of kinship abreast his soul. It was a primitive obsession, a primitive disease, an obsession with sight and execution, sacrificial constellation.

The priests had supported him in the camouflage of the ant but they warned him against his new venture, ship of scale. It might prove precipitate and dangerous but Quiyumucon hardened his will.

He put his men to work and soon the hatred of the enemy turned to amazement though the intention of it all – such amazing craftmanship – they could not fathom: it was not the alien Horse of Troy nor the fiery Cross of Spain which rose to confront them but a fleet of Magical Canoes built with infinite skill like a fantastic rehearsal of a play of sacrificial rocks – blind man's ford – in the cave of dreams. Except that at this stage of rehearsal in the migration of the Caribs – valley of creation – the mastheads chosen were neither those of Poli nor the warrior maiden though, in fact, the mountains stood overhead in anticipation of a future voyage back into the paint of the sun and the valley itself in which the vessels grew, deck by deck, line by line, was like a giant ship itself or lap of war.

There were, first of all front-line vessels of the jaguar, so built they appeared ready to spring at a moment's silence. They were moored to a trigger of rock. And sometimes in the starved watercourse where they lay like vertical horizons or sprung hammocks weighing the sky, the slip knot of lightning stiffened at either end presaging the fixed rains to come across the valley of time.

In the second line stood vessels of the forest so built they looked like trees ready to walk, to blossom fire at a moment's silence. They were moored to skeleton rock. And sometimes in the starved watercourse where they stood, they leaned like the charmed antlers of the land festooned with fossil palm and the rust of orchids presaging the fixed hail to come across the valley of time.

In the third line stood vessels of cloud so built they looked like birds of storm ready to fly at a moment's silence. They were moored to the cloud of rock. And sometimes in the starved watercourse where they rested they looked like the silent race of the wind whose spirit of evaporation was the quicksilver of action presaging the fixed vapour to come across the valley of time.

In the fourth and last line stood vessels of the fish so built they looked like the very scales of earth. And these – unlike the first three lines which were sparked to spring however still the dream of action – were anchored to the very heart of unconsciousness (earth's dive or motion) presaging an ocean of space to come though the fixed rains ran and the fixed hail fell and the fixed vapour blew.

As the four lines of the fleet appeared the enemy looked and wondered but could not fathom their relative function and intention. Yet they were held, as it were, by the hand of magic as though the moorings which held the various craft drew them, too, into orbit, fixture of rain and hail and cloud. It was an elaborate and compelling mission of beauty and skill.

They were aware all the time – during the spell of construction – that such a fleet could not dream to embark until the river rose to its full height. Quiyumucon read their hearts, First Tenants of the Land. He knew they would bide their time, fiends nursing ambition, until the vessels were finished. Then they would descend, armed to the teeth, to appropriate the spoil: such wealth as they had never imagined – the fixed boat of creation – beasts, forests, clouds, birds – the fleet of time.

Quiyumucon knew, as one conversant with the deeds of the sky, the very hour the river would rise and the elements come. He set his trap and the enemy, dumbfounded at their opportunity – everything ready and finished now – began to descend into the river.

Quiyumucon, safely positioning himself on the mountains of heaven, laid his ritual charge of sunrise, explosive hail, rain, wind, to the masthead of Poli, the ship of the valley. The priests sought to restrain him but he was adamant. It was a sacred mountain, they said, born of the sky and the maiden of earth. It was First Cause, they said. But Quiyumucon hardened his heart against them all, sacred and profane, conflicting causes. He was determined to trigger his fleet, sacrificial enemy in friend, tenant's hand within tenant, crew of originality in time… *and set sail…*

As the First Tenants of the valley (as the enemy called themselves) boarded creation's camouflage Quiyumucon struck. Some say it was not he, after all, whose dive into silence it was but a god's hail of the fathomless moorings and lightning of man.

Others, that it was a god's rain of the swiftest sound and music of man, unplumbed earth, in which the stillest fleet set sail.

Whatever it was Quiyumucon had not been misled by the oracles of despatch through the spoil of war.

The priests said it was his act of disobedience which matched everything, lightning and sound, rain and hail, masthead of the deeps, sea of silence – but he (Quiyumucon) believed it was sight and execution, spirit and intention rolled into one primitive configuration.

As the masthead of Poli snapped and fell Quiyumucon waited, knowing it all already in his heart like the lance of a dream: the new hands he had enlisted in his fleet.

As the first rubble of the deed of the sky fell he saw the first line of vessels stir. The enemy on the deck were so astonished they grew dumb with fascination akin to the beasts they rode and this concert or trigger nerved them to spring on the lance-head of the jaguar through their own gloating plot or desire for the spoil of earth.

Quiyumucon waited and watched. It was a propitious sacrifice, a propitious beginning and end to greed and cruelty. As the second wave and rubble of the deed of the sky fell he saw the second line of his fleet stir and the antlers or vessels of the forests sprang like horns of silence upon which the bodies of the enemy grew still beyond every semblance of desire. It was a passive ornamentation of the hand of his fleet like a caveat of soul in the heart of the future.

Quiyumucon waited and watched. As the third wave or rubble from the deed of the sky fell he saw the third line of his fleet stir like the quicksilver of storm whose annihilation of the lusts of spoil – birds of storm – froze their blood at the same time into a rain of silver wrought upon the wing of each ship. It was a mute cloak or extension into a new world, silent as the gleam of tears.

Quiyumucon waited and watched. As the fourth and last wave fell, the last of his vessels stirred. And now it was as if fire itself broke loose within every hand, clock of sacrifice, but, in fact, the vessels of this line, beyond all others, were chained to death, the endless death of death, the endless beginning of beginnings. Chained therefore to life, link of reflection, Carib boat of the unconscious.

As the massive deluge charged – across line upon line of ship, electric creation – the earth-fish dived and stood, scale of rain, scale of cloud like a knife-edged balance within the rage of the spoil, fused enemy and friend, spiritual tenant...

I woke now in the eye of the Quiyumucon sun which streamed into the cave.

YUKOKON

NOTE

Yurokon *serves in this story as a gateway between Carib★ and Christian ages. His appearance as the Bush Baby in Carib mythology – the child of the vessel (the Caribs are noted for their beautiful pottery) – coincided both with a fall from sovereign time and dominion, and with the arrival of Columbus.*

The charges of cannibalism levelled against them by Spain, whom they resisted fiercely step by step, appear to have been trumped up by her to justify her own excesses and to be largely untrue, though it is clear from mythological relics such as bone or flute, fashioned from their enemies, that the Caribs ate a ritual morsel – "transubstantiation in reverse" as Michael Swan puts it.

The plastic myth of Yurokon *appears to me to possess so many hidden features (innocence as well as guilt) that I have attempted to portray it as the threshold to a catholic native within whom resides an unwritten symphony – the disintegration of idols as well as an original participation of elements.*

★ *The word "Carib" is a corruption which became synonymous with "cannibal": Columbus spoke of Caripunas, Raleigh of Carinepagotos, French explorers of Galibis.*

YUROCON

I

The Indian reservation of the valley of sleep lay in an open savannah of the Interior. Stunted bush and occasional trees dotted this savannah – miles long and wide – between the mountains where a great forest began and rolled endlessly to the sea. From this naked distance – in the middle of the valley – these forests appeared like black surf of painted cloud. Yurokon had once or twice crossed them to come to the sea. It was a far way off but his memories were intimate and vivid like newly minted letters of space, a harmony of perspectives.

The sun was up when he succeeded in raising his kite. Soon – by judicious tugs – pulling in and paying out of twine – the kite caught a current of air and rose steadily and swiftly into the sky.

He was around fourteen (so the records said); his sister, who had accompanied him, about ten. They were both small of stature, frail of limb, reputed to be amongst the last survivors of an ancient tribe now called *huntsmen of bone.* They possessed a curious air, devoid of age it seemed – animated matchsticks, smouldering a little, quiescent a little. It was the rapidity of their gestures accompanied by an inherent stillness, a silent relationship. And yet it was as if volumes of time existed between them and words of music fell ceaselessly from their lips.

They appeared now half-asleep on earth as the match of space began to slumber. And when their uncle appeared through one of the trees they were glad to relinquish the kite to him which he secured to the branch of a tree. Yurokon slid to the ground and watched uncle and sister vanish through a hump of land into the houses of the reservation.

They would return, he knew, with food and drink. He lay against the trunk of a tree and could not bear to leave his kite which he glimpsed through the leaves as it slept on a cloud – and bore him up into a skeleton of light through the valley of sleep.

"Are we really huntsmen of bone?" Yurokon asked, looking down at his uncle and through the sky as he sailed in space. For it was as if the blue trunk of the ocean stood there whittled down to a cross, coral and bone, octopus in whose blood ran tin, sponge in whose crevices ran gold.

"We became huntsmen of bone when we ate our first Spanish sailor," his uncle replied to the intricate sticks of the sky. "For that reason we are sometimes called cannibals." He looked sardonic, his left eyebrow cocked in quizzical fashion, pointing still to the kite, paper of heaven nailed to wood.

"Cannibals," said the boy, startled. "I don't see why anyone should call us that."

It was Easter in the Indian reservation of the twentieth century and Yurokon had been given a kite by a visiting missionary, which sailed through the book of space and continued in his sleep in pages of psyche; coral and gold.

"For that reason we are sometimes called cannibals," the man repeated, pursuing his own thread of thought backwards into time. "We ate a Spanish sailor…" He was jealous of the missionary and wished to distract his nephew, glued to space.

"How can you say such a thing?" Yurokon cried, descending from kite to earth in a flash and stopping dead, riveted now to the ancient trunk of man, the lines and brow, the anchor of subsistence.

They stood under a small tree in the valley of sleep and Yurokon observed a spectral nest hanging from one of its branches; to that bough also he saw had been tied the thread of his kite which he had ascended and descended on scales of light. "It's chained there," he cried as if he had forgotten whether it was the missionary or his uncle who had done it, "chained to nest and branch."

His uncle nodded to a silent tune, and reaching up into the nest drew forth a thin bone or flute. He passed it over his lips without making a sound, polished it between the palms of his hands and after this palaver with the dead gave it to Yurokon who blew, in his turn, a sad yet vibrating melody of space. All at once he could hear and feel running through his hands the giant tremor of that bird, the ladder of the pilot, as it flew soundlessly through the sky chained to the earth.

He could hear also an unwritten symphony: the dark roots in the past of that tree – a strange huddle of ancestral faces attuned to quivering wings which they plucked with their fingers like teeth. And then silently, as if for the first bitter time, tasted the fear of the strings: ascent and descent: transubstantiation of species: half-tender, half-cruel, like a feast.

They read it, in their mouths, on the craft of Spain – the curious cross of a bird which flew towards them across the sea: crane or pelican or flag. It might even have been their first fleshless pirate, skull and crossbones of the fleet, harp of flesh.

"Do you mean?" said Yurokon as the first wave of magical numbers struck him, "that it was a game to make them think they had been eaten…?" He stopped, aware of a waking plight in the valley of sleep, the plight of feeling akin to non-feeling, flesh akin to spirit.

"In a manner of speaking, yes," said his uncle approvingly. "*Make them think they had been eaten.* Make them into a song of spirit: a morsel in our mouths, nothing more, the morsel of the flute, that was all." He waved his hand nonchalantly.

Yurokon nearly spat the flute from his mouth as though suddenly it burnt his tongue like fire, immortal burn, immortal skin, immortal native, immortal cannibal. He began to age into the ancient Child of Legend. It was a story he had been told from the beginning – that he was the last Carib and the first native…

2

Yurokon appeared centuries ago in the valley of dreams as the native heaven of tears and laughter, of carnival and guilt when the revolution of conquest was over.

His uncle was expecting him and though he barely discerned the spiral of smoke like twine coming up out of the pot on the fire, he felt the sting of fire – tears of a match.

It was here in this sky of election – bastard soil – cannibal legend – that the song of the kite was born.

"Make them think it was a marriage of spirits, laughter of the feast," his uncle said languidly, with the glaze of the pot in his eye.

"I am your brother's spirit," said Yurokon and there was a responsive glaze in his mood or brow, a godlike rebellious look.

"Which one?" his uncle said flippantly to the devil of the fire. "Brother oh brother."

Yurokon bowed his head to conceal the ash of many a war feast, sculpture of blood. His uncle had many brothers – some had eaten the symbol of deity. "How can we," he said to his uncle, and the words bit his tongue, "be the first natives when they were here before us – I mean your brothers' Arawak wives – my mother's people…?"

"They're our base of time in the light of Spain," his uncle said secretively as though he reasoned with insurrection in his ranks. "No one before us has made this claim – don't you see? – this black morsel"… He stirred industriously over the cooking pot and gave a sardonic shrug. "It's our last weapon, our first election. In future, come who or what may, this distinction will stand. It will swallow us all for we, too, will succumb."

"Succumb," said Yurokon and he almost laughed at his fate. "Yet here am I," he cried accusingly, "no one and nothing, yet here I stand. Whose fault is it? Whose spirit is it that will not – *cannot* – die?"

"Child," said his uncle with a gleam that might have been fear, "it is true that the revolution of conquest is over but *you* – your rebellious feud of spirit goes on." He turned away from the glaze of the pot; the hunger of kinship was opening at his feet, twine of blood, twine of water, twine of guilt ascending and descending: flint of savage: skeleton of light.

Yurokon held the twine in his hands as if with a snap, a single fierce pull, he would break it *now* at last. Break the land. Break the sea. Break the savannah. Break the forest. Break the twig. Break the bough. The unwritten symphony of the windy unwritten spark of the wind, made him bark – a sudden bark. His uncle stared at the bristling dog of the fire, fire break, fire bark, delicacy, magic; he smacked his lips and the roast of Yurokon's bark subsided into the silent bay of conscience like an invocation at the heart of the feast: man's best enemy or friend.

Was it the immortal dog of war and peace that sang in the break of the fire, shadowy tail or bone?

Its voice could be heard in the lull of the wind across the valley of sleep. First the subtlest crash of a symphony, staccato fire, forest tail or bay of the moon in the sky.

Second a hoarse thump which came from a falling tree, surf or tail of the moon.

It was the music of ignominy, ignominious conceit, or so it seemed to Yurokon (his own desire to break everything) on his long march across time into the rebellion of eternity. A long march in which the tail of his kite drew a line across the ash of the sky, camp fire or ghost settlement. A line of demarcation, the frontier of sleep, huntsmen of bone, the song of silence.

It was equally the music of origins upon a trail that lay in all the wild warring elements. First, *broken water*. His uncle possessed an enormous cauldron which he filled with water and set on the fire. Yurokon beheld the dog of his skin soon bubbling there like a cataract of eternity: boiling water which had been innocent before – innocent, that is, as one's own sovereign blood, but now had become the executioner at the feast, native to blood.

Second, *broken fire*. His uncle possessed an enormous spit, a cauldron of fire: as though the sun stood over the valley on a misty morning and began to break its own vessel of intensity through an autumn sunset turning into a tropical, ritual sunrise. So that the steam of the valley appeared to infuse the light, and water boiled fire rather than fire boiling water.

Yurokon saw himself aloft in this cauldron of fire as a dog-kite; the twine connecting him to earth – kite to earth – had been cut by scissors of mist. He stood, therefore, high up as if without anchor or support save that the nape of his neck had been caught by fingers of fire: fingers of a god which had been innocent before – innocent as one's sovereign flesh, but now had become an executioner at the feast, native to flesh.

At this moment on the trail beholding water and broken fire, he looked backwards and forwards at the combat of heaven: immortal outcast, outcast of participation, innocence and guilt. Heaven lay both within and without the things and the people he had taken for granted, and the kite of deity had, on one hand, consolidated – as uncle hinted – a base of time, an election of time to swallow all ages and men; but, on the other, had equally inspired a curious break within the anatomy of the feast – a spiritual hunger and rebellion whose consequences would reveal the inmost vessel or nativity of fate, song of fate.

He had passed through broken voices of water and fire. Now broken atmosphere lay before him like the breath on his lips fried thin as a wafer, flat as a leaf. And so when he moved he began to fly with the feud of air into broken distances: broken water and fire cooked into walls of space by leaves of wood as though water and fire were cold and wood and leaf were hot: wood and leaf which had been innocent before – innocent as nature, but now had become the kite of distance, native to sovereign execution, death-in-life, life-in-death.

Fire. Water. Air. They were all, in a sense, the weapons of a savage dreaming time on a trail where *once upon a child* everything had slumbered on a leash like a victorious shroud but now had become the cauldron of heaven which the huntsmen of bone had not foreseen when they appointed themselves the cannibal or ogre of place to fashion both their catholic native and repulsive sack of the seasons.

That the leash would become the easter twine of endless participation through an immortal outcast, and that the repulsive stocking or sack of the seasons would invoke stomach upon stomach of consumption whose hideousness would be reflected in a deeper and deeper childlike pool of innocence (ogre of water, boiling fire) – raw material of the elements – none had foreseen as the undying birth of freedom…

For it was as if – just as angelic blood was consumed by cannibal water – fire by an atrocity of wood – broken savage time lay, too, within its native soil eternity.

Yurokon was approaching a bend in the trail and he saw both

the shroud and sack of the seasons before him. The shroud may well have been a caul such as certain children are born with. The sack or stocking may well have been the pillow of conquest, Eiger in Roraima, snow of the Alps in the Andes in the Amazon. He could now hear the gift of a symphony in the silent bed of earth – black-out shroud of vision, white-out stocking of translation. He had heard the missionary on the reservation speak of the Polar North as an organ of fire it was so cold. Yurokon believed and accepted this paradoxical truth as much as he trusted the song of himself in the sorrow of the bone and the flute – the ages of man – valley of desolation.

"Once upon a child," the shroud said to him advancing along the trail like the dance of the black keys of earth.

"Once upon a time," the sack said to him advancing along the trail like the dance of the white bones of earth.

Yurokon hopped to the white bone and the black flute. He could see clearly now, with the eye of his kite, the ballet of the Caribs as they stubbornly withdrew within the music of the centuries upon the skull-and-crossbones piano of age. At each camp fire they grew extinct in the ash of reflection, but were born again within involuntary pillow or shroud, caul of vision.

Yurokon stepped upon these keys of birth-in-death – broken water and broken fire – black-out... white-out... ash of earth which he rode like a ladder into the sky.

3

The ladder of the trail ran up into the mountains. And each day as the Caribs withdrew into the clock of the centuries they painted the blue sea falling away beneath them in an under-world picture, an underworld kite which flew in the broken sky of conquest. Flew under their feet upon a rope of ash which descended through knotted stations of fire where the burnt relic of each day's march was buried. It burnt itself there – imagination of a continent – rope and kite – ladder of ascent, and they drew the sea upon their pots and vessels – something fantastically small (a drop of ocean) – something immensely wide which began to consume them at the grassroots of innocence like a cauldron of fury.

The sea-kite possessed many shapes and colours, some gay, some sombre. Some – like the octopus – amused the huntsmen. It made them almost enjoy the innocent malady of the gods since unholy, holy evil was reputed to have a stomach of mail which drank tin.

"Once upon a child," said the stomach of mail to the conscience of the tribe, namely Yurokon, "you ate me," and it tangled its tail and rope around him on the ladder. His uncle laughed, and his sister, taking pity on him, grabbed the octopus by the bones of the kite and ran a little way off across a wave of land to give him room to coax it back into the air.

Another kite, which rose in the underworld sky at his feet, resembled a sponge and this, too, was an endless model of diversion. When the battle of conscience drew it, infinite drops of gold splashed on the ground from the heart of the pelican.

"Once upon a time," said the sponge to the pelican, "I flew in the sea with wings of bone."

In addition to the kite of the octopus and the kite of the sponge there flew a kite of coral, a submerged reef crossed with ritual cousins, related to the sponge, calendrical mosaic, music. It curved and dwindled in shallows and deeps, skeleton of the sea, harp of the feast from which a stringed sound issued, fossil of cloud.

Far beneath the ladder of the mountains the ocean crawled within itself, ribs of bone splashed by huntsmen of shadow. Yurokon observed in the middle of that kite of ocean a loop of burning paint. This was the cauldron of the kite within which octopus and coral and sponge, innocent evil and maleficent good, were living morsels of divinity in their native organ. The laughter dried on his lips – flute of bone – and he tasted instead plankton or euphausiid harnessed to blood: harnessed to the urchin of the sea, spiked hedgehog or jealous god of ocean. This spiky pattern upon the cauldron of the kite reflected the jealous sky of the sea – the brittle constellations and stars, prickly sea-lilies, sea-cucumbers set in a mosaic of fossil and keyboard of ancestors. As though the spiky music of the urchin of stars, the election of thc first native of earth, drew one deeper and deeper into a furnace of innocence, consumption of guilt.

Yurokon was the hedgehog of the land, Carib land-urchin to Spanish sea-urchin. He could bark and bristle on the land as if fire were his natural element, sea-dog of night, and with the fall of darkness he no longer flew the sea-kite under him, but rather the land-kite over him.

He imagined himself standing upon the shore of the sea with a new boatload of arrivals, looking up with their eyes at a distant camp fire of Caribs. The ground was strewn with the dead of battle, but the bone of the kite blazing on the mountains spoke volumes of the savage character of the land, dancing around its flute. It was as if the dance of the bone wished to declare itself after a day of battle – to all who had newly arrived – by a music of silence, spirit of absorption, gaol of flesh.

That absorption reflected the many shapeless kites of Yurokon in the heart of invader as well as invaded. There was the night octopus of the land whose dance differed from the tail of the sea in that the daytime octopus was a morsel of divinity, morsel of the sea, but the night-time octopus, as it blazed its points far up on the ladder of the land, seemed the very antithesis of the gods: land-urchin's shroud or sack: camp fire of bone: trunk or tree on which Yurokon laid his head in the valley of sleep. Each splinter of the dance, seen from the foot of the cross, ladder of the mountains, flared in the match of a dream, matchstick limbs, twine and distance: glimmer of the pointed hedgehog.

4

Yurokon's field was the grain of the land and sea whose seed-time was conscience, battle of eternity.

As the Caribs withdrew across the ridge of the land and began to descend into a continent of shadow, each knot of ash linked them to the enemy. And Yurokon was the scarred urchin of dreams, victor-in-victim; over the centuries he remained unageing (ageless) as a legend, a curious symptom or holocaust of memory, whose burnt-out stations were equally embryonic as a cradle, fugue of man, unchained chain of fires.

It was this that drew the Caribs to the end of their age. They ceased to fret about names since namelessness was a sea of names. They ceased, too, to care about dwindling numbers since numberlessness was native to heaven, stars beyond reckoning.

The tree, in fact, against which Yurokon slept was known as the tree of name and number. And there were two paths which led to it from the mountains around the valley. The first was called *the ladder of the geese.* It was a game Yurokon had designed in which he dreamt it was all happening the other way around. The mountains were paper – flat as a map. The valley was above, sailing kite, and the barnacle geese which flew towards him rose from paper to kite: hatched not from eggs like other birds but from sea-shell into land-fish, orphans of the globe. For they, too, like Yurokon, were an ageless omen, Good Friday's meat, fish rather than fowl. None grieved for them save Yurokon who accounted himself sibling to a shell – sibling to a fast – as uncle accounted himself guardian to a morsel.

It was the true name of the geese, the true number of the fast which baffled all men. Yurokon drew the flight of the geese as currents or arrows against the shadow of continents – gulf stream or orphan of masses, equatorial current or orphan of hemispheres.

"Barnacle currents," he thought. Wing by fin the land-fish flew – the souls of a drought, the fast of the drowned – waters under the earth.

The valley of sleep had been taken by assault – the fiercest savannah fire of living memory; so swift had it been, all were killed who were taken unawares. Stunted trees remained – bones of grass. Uncle had died, as had Yurokon, in the glare of battle. And now – after three or four years – the scene was revisited by the Catholic missionary of the Interior, Father Gabriel. It was he who encircled on a map the charred tree of Yurokon as a new root or mission of psyche, spectral nest, bone and flute: it was Eastertide again.

He had visited the mission and given Yurokon a kite two days before the blaze – had he remained he, too, might have been killed. Now here he was again to make a new start, both defend and attack from within and without. An unorthodox priest he was of Spanish and Indian blood, and a composer of music. He dreamt of a native symphony which would reflect a new organ or capacity, a primitive flowering of faith. It was not inconsistent with the last dream of the Caribs, the dream of Yurokon which haunted him, as it haunted them – annunciation of music at the beginning of the end of an age.

"Sailor," said Yurokon to Gabriel. The priest began to protest. But his voice was muffled in his cloth or vocation. He wanted to say – "I am not your mask or morsel." But instead – like curtain and theatre – he let the faceless robe of God descend; Yurokon set aside the flute from his lips and placed collar or shell to his ear.

There were two ladders (Yurokon remembered) leading to the robe of name and number. The first called tree of the barnacle goose, the second simply *hemispheres: shell of the spheres.*

Yurokon kept the shell to his ear until arrows of rain evoked an abstract pitch, volume within line. The music he now heard was both hollow and full, sea-fast, land-fast. When the sea fasted, it still climbed into the rain of the land: land-fish, Good Friday's arrow.

Yurokon could hear her sing – his sister who ran before him now through the day of the battle of the savannah – arrow of fire – when mail or flame swept on. As though in the singing theatre of God, history re-enacted itself...

The fire voices came from everywhere and Yurokon woke to the voice of the tree in which he slept.

He was rooted, in that moment, in fire – as his sister ran before him with the singing kite of the savannah – fiery attack, fiery defence.

In the grain of that field of battle – open to conscience – open to sun – an omen resided, multiplications of grace, zero as well as fulfilment. This was the logic of Father Gabriel – the open book of the centuries: annunciation of the native of the globe.

And now – as his sister ran before him – Yurokon saw a chain of fires (formerly ash, unchained chain of divinity) but linked or aligned to him now beneath his robe.

He recalled the naked campfires of his forebears whose arrows swarmed on the brink of a continent like currents of ocean barnacled to land.

They were lit, he remembered, as the first grim tide of welcome to the flag of the pelican. They were equally an offensive/defensive swarm, blazing at the door of the land – sponge of the sea – blood of gold: blazing ribbon of coastline, legend or sponge.

He recalled the fierce battles that raged day after day; the retreat that followed night after night, the fatalistic withdrawal into hedgehog and mountain.

The chain of fires along the roof of the coast was the first curiously horizontal phase, therefore, in a vertical war – a vertical cloak or retreat which Yurokon encompassed at this stage as the shroud of the land-urchin over the sea-urchin, land-kite over the sea-kite, night over day.

It was a slow and long pull, he recalled, from the sea to the crest of the land, but they drew their train after them up the mountains, braced themselves in the current of the wind, wing to fin, bone to sack, goose to hemisphere – fast of name and number, tree of camouflage, feast of camouflage, trail of campfires in a single line or uninterrupted break of terror.

One last crackling glance back at the sea-kite from the sky-ridge of the mountains where they stood; he could see them again as they leaned forward, reluctant, sad, and drank a toast (farewell to namesake sea) lip to bowl, lip to the engraving of Spain (and all who came after, bowl of England, saucer of France, vessel of Holland): they engraved it on their lips – primitive fire or callous – like an animal's protuberance, mouth of the sun whose tongue ran with them as they descended the other flank of the mountains – away from the sea – into the lap of the land.

Half-way down they looked back with Yurokon's eyes, and saw her standing there – Sister Fire – Viking Amazon. Her eyes met theirs as she turned from the flank of the sea to the cloth of land. And this time Yurokon felt the parenthesis of the orphan, sea-shell into robe.

Every protection, nevertheless, seemed precarious to him now as the battle of ridge and flank, forest and savannah rolled on: as though his own sister possessed a chain of ambivalences – a menacing outwardness as well as inwardness, unearthly stillness chained to storm, locked propensity, locked voices of fury.

He could see them – his forebears of bone – with their chain of flesh and spirit across the land. They had crossed the naked flank of the sea into the vessel of the forest and now – as they descended into species of Bush and Savannah – Yurokon was aware of the intensity of the flame they drew with them, which like vase or pottery in a rage of colour, signified an acute vice in themselves, blaze or furnace.

He had never been aware of it quite so strangely before – the flimsy scaffold of the robe, shroud of name and number, urchin of the stars, caul of birth, which – like ash – night-kite over day-kite, could mercifully fall to release the chain; or like earth, in the hands of a wise potter, could unlock the vice; but which (in the fold of that vice, colour of fire) broke, for no other clear reason but to instil terror: as if – in breaking – it had not broken at all, save to clinch an outer flesh to an inner mould, an outer fire to an inner blow.

It was this inner blow which, despite the appearances of hell, drew Yurokon back to prize the ash – not as the holocaust it seemed to be, but as the robe of mercy it originally was, parenthesis of the orphan.

Nevertheless, in withdrawing there, he could still see – within his own glimmering shadow – that the chain of the battle rolled on; the fire voice of the savannah sang close at hand of the flesh and spirit of the tiger which had been joined to withstand (within and without) forces and enemies.

And the voice of the tiger, fire voice, fire vase – in line with sea-flame, mountain flesh, muse of the ridge, toast of ancestors, penetration of flank – instilled terror. And like an apparition of ancient camp fire, it disported its robe or ash, bars of shadow through which its naked sides shone: insane factory of war: jointed engine of battles upon which the cloth of the priest precariously stood – not as the sport of unfreedom, but as a necessary condition, leash of grace.

It was curious (half-comic perhaps, half-tragic perhaps) that, in a sense, this ash (this prison) was the flimsy sponge of nature which alone drank volumes of need; the ill-protected, the ill-served – true voice of the tiger.

True voice of the tiger. It began to sing now with rage and scorn: rage at the conversion of prison: scorn at the factory of grace. And as it sang – in repudiation of the ash of truth – its rage and its scorn were joined to flesh and spirit.

This was the last chain, last repulse of the Caribs in that battle of the savannah, whose commemoration rose in a vase of flame: such music of colour it embroiled the savannah in the sea, the mountain in the valley, forest in scrub: bowl of earth, pottery of earth, toast of the valley by the huntsmen of bone who had drunk before from the bowl of the sea.

Such commemoration of colour – such a draught of sensation – such a feast of sensibility – embroiled all things and species in a breakwater of reflection, stretching from the harp of the sea to the kite of the valley.

That music of paradox began with a bar of shadow – unchained fire – *hiatus* of ordeal as the robe of God, the need of man; followed, however, by the wildest repudiation of that need in the sack of truth: though this very sack or body of rage began to point again, back to itself as to an ironical witness, an unremembered, unacknowledged sibling of truth on both sides of the veil.

For if, in fact, the inner tiger of war repudiated its veil or shadow, there were other species whose storm or sack drew them back without protest to the spirit of placelessness, as to the salt of the sea.

The eel of fire, for example, as it ran into battle, coiled into an eye of relief which could have been a needle of snow. For eye of snow, like barnacle of fire, legendary feather, had been spawned on a distant scaffold – desert or Pole – where it grew like an arrow from a subtle hand mapping the globe.

The bird of species as well, as it flew into battle, spun the feather or the thread in the needle in the very eye of snow. For the thread of the needle (eye of snow) had its loom on an indifferent scaffold – North or South – whose seamless fire was a *different* shadow, cloth over the Pole.

Yurokon spied that cloth – East, West – as it sailed on high beneath and above sister and uncle. Sailed on high, composite bird, flower, tailed beast; sailed in the spiral of the winds as he tugged gently, pulling in, paying out his twine with masterly skill. He was the child of legend and the lord of creation and his paper or map, kite or globe, was a magical witness of curious survival, the terrifying innocent play of a timeless element in all places and things. In all its manifestations it seemed to Yurokon to spell relief at the summit of his need.

His small sister, running before him, began to sing to the kite with joy.

"Eastertide again," Father Gabriel said to himself, "annunciation of music."

THE AGE OF THE RAINMAKERS

For Margaret and Tony
and to the memory of James Glasford

Originality is the fragile yet indestructible arch of community whose web is akin to but other than space.

– Rainmaker's Epitaph

THE AGE OF KAIE

NOTE

The twins of rain and drought – as certain vestiges of Macusi legend imply – are instinctive to the symbolism of the Guianas and Brazil – to great spirit Makonaima and great ancestor Kaie.

I have attempted in this story to interpret the rainmaking fabric of the Macusis as a conception of opposites which has largely been obliterated by histories of conquest – Carib, Spanish, French, English, etc.

Paterson, the half-caste twentieth-century revolutionary, becomes – in this fable – an intimate extension of ancestor Kaie in a long line of guerrilla camouflage – stone-flower of the conquistador. Young Kaie is mortally wounded fighting beside him.

The broken fabric of Macusi legend conceals its true scale – in relating animal features to the gods – and may never have possessed, from the very beginning, an exclusive sum of visual characteristics.

A musical dialogue in nature may be closer to the mysterious ruin of hunter and hunted which is all we possess now like a ballet of the species, and this brings into a different and subtler focus the reeling dance of the dreaded bat of Makonaima – to take one peculiar example – whose fantastic ultrasonic rapport with creatures on land and under water, as it flies through the air, has begun to occupy the mind of art and science as complex iconography akin to a genuine opus or spectre of need whatever assumptions of diabolical appetite are associated with it.

I have attempted in this fable – through an accumulation of particulars bordering upon self-revelation/self-deception – to draw as close as I can to the sacrificial momentum of Kaieteur Fall as icon or caveat wherein ancestor Kaie, in concert with Makonaima's self-generating brood of elements (tree, animal, etc.), broke the drought overshadowing his people.

The Age of Kaie *may be read as a story in its own right but it gains in focus, I believe, when reconsidered as part of the entire context of* The Age of the Rainmakers. *For it is related to a certain drama of consciousness incorporating compensatory roles of the evaporation as well as precipitation of the spirits of the tribe.*

Each successive story in this volume looks back to The Age of Kaie *in some particular way that may enhance a certain train of associations and* Arawak Horizon, *the last story, serves to condense an overlap between the absence and presence of gods in history through ironical furnitures or economic omens.*

ONE

1

Roraima and Kaieteur are the fabric of a curious gateway into South America north of and almost parallel to the dust of the Equator: drenched in sleep and cloud – shot through again by imminent distances like floating unruly perspectives in the wake of an expedition.

"Gateway of legend," Paterson said to Kaie, the young Macusi warrior who lay dying at his side, "and though it appears sometimes easy to enter, at other times – even when one's inside – it feels shut in one's face like mathematics of cloud and sky. Or if not shut," he added wryly, "full of pitfalls and contours as though subject to dreaming ores (inside/out, outside/in) which swing the needle of one's compass from pole to pole. What a jump, Kaie," and he laughed. "Perhaps we do it all the time without knowing. We jump…" He caught his breath sharply as the pain stabbed. "Jump where and with what?" asked Kaie.

"With the pole of the elements into other creatures and ages, magnetic pasts and futures." He laughed chokingly and shrugged half at himself, half at Kaie; then with an effort lifted himself on an elbow which grew now beneath him into something more than the mere stump of fate; shook his wrist like a compass; lifted two fingers to eye, took aim and bearing on the game of space far across the plateau – sky of the mountains. As he held the hallucinated compass and discerned a whirl of numbers, exploding stars, he could hear again – as if it were all happening at this very moment – a burst of fire from the direction of the waterfall.

The rain began to fall but on second thoughts he said to Kaie – "Not rain – blood." Then he remembered: the torn waterfall of creation pounding on the rocks like mute cannon of an archaic legend sometimes blew its echo or spray (they seemed indistinguishable) far across the land – paint of the sun raining a mythical aspect of landscape which sometimes rose into the wounded guardian of the gate. It was here on this very ground that government troops had appeared and fired with eccentric guns – machines of space – at a parcel of rebellious primitives, Paterson's Indians. Paterson saw them as a parcel – his poor guerrilla bands of time – because as they fled a large sheet of paper wrapped around him, half-vapour, half-cloud, split down the middle and they tumbled out of his side. Tumbled out of his paper into the epitaph of space.

Kaie and Paterson had been hit, others killed outright as the party scattered. Loss of blood gave them (Paterson and Kaie) this sensation of paper and space as if they shared the same interior, the same echoing body of fragmentary particulars, and the elements were hallucinated within them and without.

Kaie was aware that Paterson was elated, common-or-garden camouflage, god's paper of space: the *naiveté* of revolutionary fatherhood. The others, he knew, who escaped unhurt, had scattered – in keeping with previous instructions – in twos and threes – some up to the mountains to blend, as it were, into a mosaic of cloud; some into Brazilian rivers to blend, as it were, into a mosaic of water; some into caves to blend, as it were, into a mosaic of rock.

Through a fringe of bush where they lay on the ground they dreamt they could reach out and touch the mountains. If they could gain those, Kaie felt, they would be safe for a while but how could they make it when enemy troops were patrolling...

"Might as well walk in air, in space," Paterson said and fell back with a sense of drought. It began to dawn on him in his broken frame of mind – fertile resemblances (Indian tree, sky, water, rock) fathered by drought – that the parent of revolution was itself the offspring of deficiency which *he* (Paterson) had witnessed in the paint of the sun like food of memory.

Was this debilitation of premises (blood-bank of space) an extension of the death of the gods into the fabric of revolution?

"Our enemies," said Paterson hypnotically as he lay dying, "are *our* fierce nostalgic creation, *our* hope of compensation, *our* hope

110

of heaven or hell. We who are weak create what is strong. We bend our last gasp to the creation of the enemy – as our own guard – patrol of immortality…"

His voice rose and fell with hollow flippancy – hollow self-mockery – to which suddenly there came an answering cry like a long-dead echo, ancestor Kaie – cat or bird mewing to the conquistador of heaven. And Paterson had the curious ironic sensation that in the hollow pit of his body – ancestral Indian enemy – Kaie's breath had been caged for centuries instinctive to the residue of legend – betrothal of opposites. Kaie felt now as if he were looking through Paterson across the long drought of an age within which the dust of initiation rippled again and swirled again upon a canvas familiar with ruin, endless marches, counter-marches, patrols.

Often in the past they had lain like this side by side – drunk with the glory of hope akin to despair like soldiers on a spree – a giant spree – *Drink Deep – Drink Death*. Kaie choked as if the dust were settling in his throat, choked as Paterson laughed and clapped him on the back.

"A great drought," Paterson confessed, "when your namesake or ancestor was taken prisoner. He was called king of the house of betrothal – of the hollow maiden of the tribe." He laughed still as he clapped Kaie on the back. Then suddenly as if to push him *there* – back into the past – archaic skeleton – he cried, "Quick. Lie still, the patrol's coming." Kaie fell flat on mother earth and kissed the ground as if it were the bride of the gods. He could hear the tramp of the patrol going past perhaps twenty feet away. It was curious but as they passed the thick drapery of the bush estab-lished an illusion of distance (as if twenty paces were a thousand years or as if each echoing boot pushed him down into the cradle or the grave).

"It's true," said Paterson and whistled the bird-song of the Macusis under his breath. "The distances of history melt or multiply with each convertible echo." Kaie nodded lifting his eyes now to the colour of the sun which seemed to clothe the skeleton of history with a diffused radiance or waterfall of leaves; as the sounding step of the patrol faded the echo of his breath, caged in Paterson, died in unison with it and Kaie dreamt – as his senses ebbed and flowed – that he stood within a great hollow body scooped from the guerrilla of ages into a new maiden architecture of place. Scooped and dispersed at the same time into a savage/tender carpet painted with a waterfall of seasons – suns, moons, days, nights – upon which every young warrior of the tribe, from the beginning of ancestors, slept with the maiden of his choice ringed closely by a patrolling design of the enemy whose fists were her breasts, taut and green and poised.

Within that maiden architecture – house of betrothal – a single star shone, as night began to fall, against which loomed, at first faint then clearer by degrees, the shadow of the enemy scout and Kaie saw, with his heart in his mouth, that a single member of the cunning ring on patrol had returned across the plateau and noiselessly bore down on him. Without a word they grappled – heartbeat of the enemy – initiation of love – the beginning of a long secret corridor within the hollow maiden of the tribe (stone-flower of the conquistador) which would lead – if all went well – through darknesses like conflagrations to the treaty of the sun.

Her breasts, the enemy's fists, sent him reeling but they closed again and this time he stabbed. The enemy crumpled and Kaie sank to his knees with the sense that he had unwittingly reopened a wound, an ancient wound it seemed he remembered receiving himself a long, long time ago… He began to clean the blade of his knife until the friction of cloth on metal – like flesh in stone – became as subtle as the ruin of life, dead scout, endless bride.

2

It was this subtle voice coming it seemed from the bride of the forest which attuned him to the renewal of mortal danger. He ceased wiping the blade of his knife but the grating sound addressed him still – a whisper of cork drawn around the rim of the world, glass of earth. *Someone was coming.* It had an instanta-

112

neous effect. His senses reeled like a moth to a tune – baton of Makonaima.

The star on the carpet in the house of betrothal vanished and a misty half-moon, half-wing steeped everything. At any moment, Kaie knew, the next dreaded scout might loom larger and darker than his predecessor.

There was a drought over the land and the wine-soaked cork of the jungle reflected a mirage or feast – spectre of famine – a decline in the volume of the river threading its way on the thinnest wire of sound.

It seemed incongruous and yet fitting that the blade with which he had killed one man had now been refined on its loom into a single wire or thread intimating the dress of all things: the dress of trees like fantastic-looking boulders in waterfall or river: the dress of famine like an unsealed bottle in the hollow of his ribs, *her* ribs, too, the maiden of the tribe. It filled him with rage and tenderness, foreboding and terror as he waited for the thread of glass to unwind itself afresh – vine, snake or creeper, claw or bat of the moon.

Kaie saw it closing in on him; he thrust the dead scout in his side towards the claw of the patrol, half-wing of darkness, half-hood of light. And the bat or patrol which flew towards him suddenly stopped in its tracks, conscious all of a sudden that its own blood had been spilled, its own familiar ruin or face; it hovered there for an instant as if the threads of love and death, flesh and spirit had crossed: then deciding swiftly to leave Kaie alone and take the other tangible reflection, caught the dripping bottle he had flung – caught it securely as Kaie caught her, the hollow tribe of his soul. As it withdrew with the dregs from the bottle on its lips, it sealed a kiss, betrothal of opposites, wine of the feast, mirage, celebration, thread of famine, thread of reality, thread of cosmos: sealed it within a capacity to unravel its own patrol of subsistence, its own remorseless self-consumption, appetite for fear, doom, revolution, echo of solipsis.

The house of betrothal – ground of Makonaima – stretched from an inconspicuous seed to an inconspicuous sound – birth of lightning to seal of thunder. The tree of rain grew to enfold it (that house of the maiden) and the women of the Macusis dreamt they could measure the sum of its parts by relating Kaie (man-seed) to a flower or guardian at their gate; others to a drought or jealous god at their gate.

They brought their separate vessels, therefore, to the door of the hollow maiden of the tribe with whom Kaie slept.

Slept, as it were, with the ear of his heart to the shell of the ground – inconspicuous seed to inconspicuous sound. He could hear the feet of the vessels – ring of feminine mould – where before there had been a concert of masculine stones – enemy patrol. As though in some curious way each ancient stone guarding the gate to the house of betrothal was unsealed now – unstoppered now into a pact between mass and hollow, flesh and spirit, nature and psyche – extending over the centuries like the architecture of a new age compounding love and war – violence and fate – into the *caveat* of form. With the death of Paterson (half-caste modern revolutionary) it was as if a long-standing drought issuing from the very patriarch of guerrillas – stone-flower of the conquistador – became the anatomy of conquest unsealed now as the new feminine guardian of the gate darkening in a flash into a gigantic rose or waterfall descending towards them – hollow maiden of the tribe with whom Kaie slept in a rainmaking betrothal fashioned from need – their need to reconcile the twin elements. He could hear the fall of each petal as it settled into the patrol of the centuries carven from the stone-flower of the conquistador. On his first encounter with the twin shadow of the enemy he had been smitten by drought fists, green breasts; on his second encounter he had thrust the shadow of death from him, the echo of solipsis; now it was the anatomy of lightning fury guarding his gate in the name of conquest which began to assault him like an accumulation of tyrannies associated with the hollow deeds of man encircled by the arms of woman...

He dreamt he moved in secret file down the brow of a pass, throat, lips of the conquistador – ambush or maiden. When the stroke fell they drew together, man to man, Kaie to maiden, like fingers on one hand. Five in all each shod in his separate callous. It rested there – that hand of god – upon its pass of love or death. *Kaie recalled it clearly:* it was his maiden engagement – his first real clash with the enemy in the body of their continent. All previous engagements faded now into mere skirmishes. Here, in the "conquistador pass" as the guerrillas christened it, lay the true maiden – the true baptism – of fire. Late in the afternoon when his own side withdrew he (Kaie) was left behind, presumed dead. He lay beside four others in fanwise formation – heads together like curious lovers kissing the ground, re-creating amongst themselves the subconscious hand of fate that had felled them from above. Kaie made the fifth finger on that hand which extended from a wrist of stone across the landscape and when the enemy patrol descended they, too, were struck by this finger (Kaie's body) crooked or twisted a little on its own shadow or trigger.

As the shadow of the patrol moved on, a bodiless hallucination possessed him – the wounded man. Not so much bodilessness as extreme isolation in association with the hand of death, extreme quick of life, extreme nail or paradox which began to compensate itself within a gigantic guardian of place reaching across the conquistador valley or maiden of earth. Reaching, as it were, from one ruined side to the other whether victor or victim, bodiless or bodily. One hand – with its giant fingers – each tall as a man – rested here on this side of eternity. The other fell there, on the other side of time, within his own retreating band of guerrillas who had stopped and out of exhaustion thrown themselves to the ground within an identical fanwise formation, heads together on a wrist of stone, limbs straight out. Except for one crooked body or finger like Kaie's on its shadow or trigger.

As he lay thus across the hollow breast of war, as if it were the maiden of the cosmos, he felt himself inwardly wrestling with the hallucinated ambivalence of one flesh extending from nail into knuckle into wrist into shoulder into death into life with such abruptness and precariousness he feared it might materialize too swiftly and cave in, as a consequence, into intimate boulders on a hill racing, all of a sudden, to the bottom of the maiden, heart of the valley.

This ambivalent fabric reflected some of the defections, treacheries, treaties, etc. wherein the conquistador pass had changed hands frequently; and yet despite it all (or because of it all) had acquired a savage mood of tenderness with each fall-out, each effort to hold or underpin the pass; so that those who departed and those who came – as within a sieve of nature – became increasingly involved in a universal spectre or solipsistic deed – boulders of war – the lightning friction of space.

A matchstick flared at this instant quick as the trigger of god across the valley like dust prickling the air to validate the drought of man within the compass of history. A sudden and prolonged thunderburst followed and Kaie saw – when it was over – that an inch of rain had fallen to scale the knuckle of the living/dead finger on the guardian of the gate.

It was late afternoon and the long shadow of that split finger – wound or psyche of the tribe – crept up the walls or fabric of the valley into antlers of metamorphosis up on the head of a bull. As Kaie reached up to grapple across space with these ridges of the conquistador, antlers of memory, antlers of patrol – he was aware of the endless tree of Makonaima (tree of the tribe) that enfolded all places and things within an iconic house of betrothal. A tree whose horns or branches seemed, on one hand, to have preserved everything intact – like the father of self-deception – in close rapport, however, with a tree whose horns of solipsis appeared to have been chopped until a matchless concert grew between mass and hollow, self-revelation, self-deception, father/mother, horned bull/hornless maiden, horned/hornless tree... *waterfall*...

TWO

3

The rain began to grow upon that hollow tree until a spectre of flood arose and the house of betrothal rocked and shuddered like a boat dragging its anchor towards a waterfall.

Kaie was filled with curious alarm. The conversion of the tree into an impending waterfall – the conversion of the house into a sacrificial boat – seemed, at first, another ruse of the enemy whose patrol he had outwitted before – rain-bottle of Makonaima, dead scout, green maiden, drought fists, quick of life, fan of memory.

But then as the chain of associations which hampered the boat, even as it released the house, ran through his hands like a ghost Kaie was aware of two anchors – not one – he had himself pulled up over the side of his vessel as it began to lift.

Two anchors – one grey, one green – lodged together. His namesake ghost, long-dead ancestor, had sown the grey one as the spectre of the flood; he, Kaie, scion of memory, had sown the green one as the bait of the flood. And one had caught the other: two ages intertwined: anchor-in-anchor, bait-in-spectre.

It was an ironic catch for as it struck the deck, arm-in-arm, bait-in-spectre, its crooked fingers arose like rescuer and rescued in the tree of the waterfall which spread now and branched in all directions.

It gave Kaie the lightning almost hilarious sensation that he had himself dived in and pulled Paterson up – in the nick of time – from the grey cloak of ancestral death which swirled around Makonaima's shoulders threaded at the same time with a sobering counterpoint – scales, knuckles – like a curious almost clerical claw, ambassadorial animal, animal of god.

On the other hand Kaie wondered whether it was he who had been rescued from green bottled depths – spectral primitive blood: swift claw, hollow revolutionary/sacrificial proportions – self-deception, self-initiation, self-absorption of deeds – which drew him back to surface across the ages within a blithe uncanny mirror antlered with grey as well as green stumps of affection.

That these stumps, which stood now on the deck of betrothal, were the hand of the god of the waterfall – the enduring spark and *caveat* of the rainmaker, anchor lodged in anchor, fist in fist, finger kissing finger – may have seemed incongruous and barren to Kaie a day or two ago, an hour or two ago, a minute or two ago but *now*, as his senses dived and returned within an associated comedy of the elements, he felt himself addressed by the ambassador of rain.

"My credentials," said the ambassador presenting his anchors.

"They look", said Kaie, "as if they've come from the bottom of the sea. Is that where your country lies – the dead of the sea?"

"Dead of the sea – yes," said the ambassador half-reflectively, half-ruefully. "That's one finger." He lifted his grey-green stumpy hand and shook it half-mockingly, half-seriously, "Here's another – dead of land. And another – dead of day. And another – dead of night. Lastly – dead of the waterfall. Five fingers in all. Do you remember now?"

Kaie was astonished. "How can you encompass…?" he began.

"I encompass *you*," said the ambassador, "on the stumps of the rain-god."

"Compass, compass," cried Paterson all of a sudden like a child stumbling in the dark, stuttering in the dark, as he sought to lift two fingers on that living/dead hand of the ambassador – two fingers like the sights of a gun across the plateau, exploding stars.

"Forked finger," said Kaie, stumbling too, stuttering too where his body arched on its lightning shadow or trigger – hand of the globe.

"Five fingers in all," said the ambassador of the rain-god raising aloft the fabric of sky and earth.

"Why do you call yourself *dead of the sea?*" asked Kaie addressing the first stump or finger on that grey-green twin anchor.

"Ah," said the stump shod in his callous, yellow callous, black skin, grey age, green youth, "I am the ring of the land around the sea: the scale of the rain, the hollow knuckle. I am the middle passage of the water-fall. See how it pours like a ghost in chains. Anchor of a slave." As the stump spoke the tree rose higher still towards its waterfall, climax, memorial.

"And why do you call yourself *dead of the land?*" Kaie spoke now with insistent breath to the second stump on that mimic hand, yellow-black chain, clanking ghost.

"Ah," said the ghost unshackling his chain, "I am the cup of the sea, the quick of the rain, dice of song. I lead the chorus of the waterfall – seedtime, harvest-time, drought-time, floodtime. Can you hear me…?"

The tree rose again, gigantic rose, hollow maiden of the waterfall whose gamble with life and death Kaie heard now – as if for the first time – like seed rattling in a cup, maiden of space.

The ambassador shook that cup and as the dice rained in the waterfall Kaie could see one eye on one face, two eyes on another, three, four, five, six which sped like cubes of cloud, wager of harvest, *die of sea, die of land.*

But Kaie was still not satisfied with the wager of the fall and he addressed himself afresh to the confusing hand of the ambassador – "One more question, ambassador – why do you call yourself *dead of day?*" His breath caught in his throat like a relentless fury.

"Coffin of rain," said the ambassador with a curious self-mocking smile. "You threw it at me, remember? I caught it…" He opened his claw and revealed the die of slavery cast upon every trail into every dangerous occupation of the future, occupation of natures, old orders, new guerrillas.

Kaie was astonished and incredulous – smitten by archaic delirium or siege, cube of the waterfall – "Shall I lie with you forever in the same black coffin?" he cried half-forgetting, half-caste revolutionary, "the same white coffin?" He paused to stroke the air – "Or do I die now in truth to resuscitate you out of fear, scout of the underworld, to throw you back my own glasshouse of necessity, lost mountains, lost rivers, lost valleys – to do with as you wish under the same assumed name – black father, black revolution, white father, white revolution, beggarman, beggar-coffin, kingman, king-coffin, son-of-man…"

The rain bowed its head into a torrent of familiars through whose thickets Kaie discerned – it seemed to him now – the self-created author of conquest; and yet something spectral, nevertheless, *incommensurable* with ruin, issued like the dust of betrothal, spirit of the fall, death of the gods, blood of man.

"Large as life now," Kaie shot back, taking advantage of this, material deed, material doggedness, triumphant at the mist of his own blood which scaled Paterson's, cloaked the sky. "I can measure you – pin you down," he cried and choked – cloud of incomprehension. "I can *measure*…" choked afresh on a sense of the monstrous deadly wager of freedom – crucifixion of the elements. The tree of his breath ascended like a thread in the waterfall as if to unravel that cloud in the coat of a universal ambassador – ambassador of the *quick* of the rain at dead of day or dead of night.

"Well, that's that," the special correspondent said, closing up his camera. "That last one should be a good shot. Funny the way these five are spread-eagled."

He lit a cigarette. In the distance he could hear the muted thunder of the waterfall punctuated by desultory firing. The last handful of rebels and the government troops fought on.

THE MIND OF AWAKAIPU

NOTE

In The Marches of El Dorado *Michael Swan speaks of the "well-documented" story of Awakaipu with mixed feelings, scepticism and belief, which reflect his own biases. Today it is becoming clearer that the kind of stoical behaviour attributed to the Indians of America north and south may reflect a complex solipsis or wishfulfilment in which explorer and explored have been involved for centuries as part and parcel of the long forlorn adventure of history.*

This solipsis became increasingly dogmatic within an apparent factuality – a partiality to fearful deeds – which overlooks inner perspectives, iconic alternatives.

The story or stories circulated about Awakaipu, the Arekuna Indian, in the nineteenth century are largely bound up I feel (some of my antecedents are Amerindian) with projections of a formal pattern – an unfeeling heroic consensus, closed plot, consolidated function or character – upon the inner breakdown of tribal peoples long subject to conquest and catastrophe.

Swan writes how Richard Schomburgk, the German explorer, "speaks in admiration of the way he (Awakaipu) behaved when attacked by perai – 'biting his lips with the raging agony he rolled about in the sand; yet no tears flowed from his eyes, no cry passed his lips'."

This kind of tale – to which has been added a sacrificial massacre performed by Awakaipu to change the skin of his race from brown to white – was common in the nineteenth century (and still is in the twentieth) as the fixed character of an age and it has endorsed the predicament of the Indian throughout the Americas. Swan himself admits that "it is a strange story with no indication of the real state of Awakaipu's mind".

It is a sombre fact that entire peoples can be conscripted within a deed to fashion the aboriginal face of a world because of a formidable hiatus – a loss of imaginative scale – at the heart of primitive realities.

The profound necessity remains therefore to begin to unravel these contradictions within oneself and, by a continuous relativizing process, extend one's horizons beyond the terrifying partiality of an age into a conception of the native as a curious host of consciousness.

This story is another venture in that direction.

GORGE OF AWAKAIPU

I caught my first glimpse of the ruin of a gorge called Awakaipu around noon. The sky was bright and yet in my dream of primitive ancestors the heavens seemed black as in some enormous painting or eclipse of the deed of the sun. When, in fact, Awakaipu himself began to loom in the canvas of that gorge he seemed the constellation not simply of darkness but of curious self-revelation: as though the brushmarks of his cradle of the sun were clearly seen now as a bright callous, a glaring misconception of nature, a blind manner or seizure by light.

I approached him and said to him – "I would like to explore the gorge…"

"Gorge!" his face grew black as if he wished now to run from me into the heart of space. "Awakaipu," I cried. "Awakaipu." I recalled the idea – akin to the gossip of an age – that to name the dead was to hold them ransom to one's will.

He stopped and looked at me with a kind of glimmering self-mockery. Like a snapshot whose ransom of history affected me now equally as it did him. As though both *name* and *will* were tools – economic tools, political tools – to purchase the negative soul of time, his as well as mine.

"What a damnable proposition," I cried. "What a damnable trap."

He looked at me and I knew he agreed.

"It's time to break out, go back…" I cried, waving towards the heart of the gorge.

I fished in my breastpocket and pulled out a bundle of newspaper clippings entitled *The Deeds of Awakaipu*. They shivered like dry leaves as if in this light they were part and parcel of an inner glow, an ironical furnace. I withdrew one of these and handed it to Awakaipu who gripped it suddenly like a clairvoyant tracing within the object he held – hieroglyphic of night – the ghostly spark of the future. Save that – with Awakaipu – the future evoked the past – one hundred calloused years ago.

"Fire years," said Awakaipu. His eyes were trembling in his mask of sleep.

So slight a tremor, however, I scarcely noticed it and was conscious that in grasping the page of the past his face seemed absolutely set – stylized pattern, ancient colour or leaf, bark of a tree. And yet once again – *there it was*: the faintest tremor quick as a vein of dust across the lid of sleep – dream of the dead, dream of the *deed* of the past as it began to reawaken from nightmare solidarity, nightmare solipsis – to reawaken and hesitantly crumble.

"Dead. Deed," I muttered. "What does it mean?"

I could hear now a sputter coming from his lips, monologue of an obsessed student repeating a lesson a hundred years ago in a laconic, unsettled order. "Code. Behaviour. Never shed a tear."

I began to watch him now as the words crackled on his lips as if coming from afar – century or centuries – to simulate a distant forest fire akin to the invention of the human voice – ancient record – ancient gramophone.

He was reputed – in the first half of the nineteenth century – to be a remarkable Indian pupil. He had learnt to read and write in German and English with a smooth rage and bloodless sophistication far in advance of his time. So much so that few dreamt he nursed a secret lapse into fear and astonishment – a staccato void – when he read an account of himself (and his own native Arekuna customs) by the German botanist and explorer with whom he worked as a guide. He noted, for example, with curious fascination that when bitten by a deadly snake he (Awakaipu) – though subject to pain – had shown implacable indifference, had rolled on the ground without a sound save the chorus of dust – crackle of limbs of earth – and never shed a tear.

"*Never shed a tear.*" As he spoke now I saw that minuscule flicker again on the dreaming mask of indifference – deed frozen upon him.

His tremor now crossed my own lids like the eye of history, reflex of history. "Deed. Dead," I dreamt and flickered as if I were the selfsame pupil, spellbound orb, character of fiction. I saw how driven I was to play in turn at senseless self-persecution, to play a role of uncanny fortitude which bordered on the inhuman, the manner of the inhuman. Never to shed a tear.

As his or my pupil flickered I dreamt the script in Awakaipu's hand was in my hand; I became Awakaipu; returned after a hundred years or more to stand outside of myself – look at myself, the stone ordeal of myself. And thus to impart to the elements something of my own native eclipse or astonishment, in the beginning, when I was cast in Awakaipu's mould.

An eclipse, on one hand, astonishment on the other that a minuscule spark of tenderness had endured to repudiate the strait-jacket of the gods – primitive pattern of hell.

I wondered whether the knowledge that I would return to stand outside of my self in a century or two – an age or two – may not have influenced my consent to entombment within a certain body or colour. Like one who knows at some stage he will inevitably turn and grope backwards into the fetishes and toys of god's childhood which have become synonymous with insensibility encompassing all his descendants on earth to such an alarming violent degree it needs to be exposed as a pathetic gloss upon immortality – upon the multifarious address of inner creative life.

My first impression – as I held the newspaper in my hand – was the manner of illustration (Awakaipu's ornaments) which I wore around my wrists – snake or albatross. A small party – including the German botanist and explorer with whom I worked as a guide – were encamped at Matope. (There are several Matopes in Guiana like a series of calendrical ghosts. For some it is the time of rapids; for others the time of mountains; for others again it is a timeless gorge – an immaterial gorge which exists as a gateway between worlds, between times.)

I rolled on the ground and I could hear now – as my own distant forest fires crackled – the rumble of my employer's voice – mechanical landslide, phonograph.

The snake which bit me, appeared, vanished so swiftly some

thought it a bushmaster, others a labaria. It had been, curiously enough, a glancing, frightened, uneasy blow – and the *piaiman* or medicine-man who accompanied the party acted almost contemptuously, extracted fang or poison and applied a cayman's tooth. I rolled on the ground nevertheless in a dead faint – overpowered more by fear than fact – inner roar of blackness, dryness in the throat, rubble of a waterfall, coal or fire, river or slide.

And so where tears rolled down heaven's cheeks before, rocks grew now at the mouth of my gorge into the nuclei of an indifferent cosmos, fortitude, tautology of the primitive, dynastic wasteland, prophetic concentration camp. I saw all this with an inner tremor of the eyelid of the dead, *dead faint,* as I clutched the dry clairvoyant paper in my hand which my employer had used a century and a half ago to press a wild flower, design or occupation of nature.

The medicine-man knelt at my side as I ceased to move and watched the faint landslide, riverslide my employer overlooked. He cupped his hands as if to shelter that flicker or die across the gamble of centuries, seminal dream, seminal tear. So faint that to overlook it was to succumb, all the more merrily, to a blind rage for inventions of historical character, factory of the deed, ordeals, substitutes, tautologies of fire, human chimney stacks as the heart of misconception – drought of tears.

It was thus that the *piaiman* counselled me as though he wished, now that an age was passing, to infiltrate my employer – to be half-employer, half-ironical-medicine priest (capital resources – psychology of the primitive).

And I – standing, as it were, within my own concert of dying/waking times, half-within, half-without the mould of Awakaipu – watched with the *piaiman* the frail lightning of immensity within the head of space he shaped with his hands which I seized upon – in the name of a stoical employer/inventor – as my first initial contradiction, solid lid, shutter of man.

Inscribed on that lid was my first collective deed or seizure of dreams – Matope of the Snake.

MATOPE OF THE SNAKE

Matope of the Snake stands at the entrance to the gorge of Awakaipu. It is a curious headland – sometimes called fist of a piaiman. Clearly it is as if the medicine-man of the tribe had indeed framed a head by cupping his hands together.

When my European employer/explorer first saw it a century and a half ago he was fascinated by this spectacle of character as he christened it.

For this headland/fistland seemed to him the cradle of a people who had banked everything into a composition of purity and greatness.

The stones were so polished they shone with the sun: so great and strong they seemed imbued in their own right with a furnace – omen of eternity.

We had set up camp there – the German botanist, the piaiman, myself and a few others. I was bitten by the half-apologetic snake of god... A glancing blow it was but enough to send me rolling on the ground, fit or faint. I dreamt the colours of earth and water, green botanist and red medicine-man, ran together and I stood, dressed in their variegated emotion, at the entrance to the under-world between the forked fingers of the universe.

I was aware, first of all, that I clung in desperation to those knuckled columns, gateway or gorge. Clung, it seemed, with bliss and courage, clown and demon: clung for a moment or two – an hour or minute in the mind of my employer – which lasted, however, in the flickering dream of the piaiman half-a-century, a full century, a century-and-a-half before it began to crackle like fire, real limbs of fire, decimation of the fires of god.

I dreamt I could read my employer's mask as never before

across the thaw of time. Read my own tribal sins as well – sacrificer and sacrificed – monument and victim – thaw of the native host of time.

As the healing thaw flickered on my Awakaipu/piaiman red eyelid I grew aware of the seminal tears of heaven as the tragic deeds of men which had congealed on the face of the gorge.

As the thaw flickered on my European green eyelid I grew aware of the gorgon of drought as a scale of resources – dewdrop sharp as a diamond – milk frozen into alabaster – shadowplay conscripted into flint.

It was this scale of atonement – red/green eyelid – I read in each seminal tear masked by the wishfulfilment of self-created things, self-created colours.

In my red eyelid had been stored a holocaust of sacrifice – a forest fire which, far back in the calendrical ghosts of creation, swept across the site of the gorge as Matope of the Snake. So swift it doubled and redoubled in its tracks, glanced this way, writhed that way. Fire-snake of ambition. I could discern it now afresh – that fire-sermon – because as the sun shone on my dead faint it glistened on the rocks with the gleam of ice until an inner thaw parted the world – and drew it together again into new attitudes, apparent totalities, fixations of longing – like an ironical magnet of landscapes, bald crowns or ages, forest spires, rock-ledges. A magnet of time that seemed to lock and unlock the sorrows and wishes of god self-inflicted by men upon men. Stone men painted red. Wood men painted red. Forest men painted red. All – my variegated population – had received that frightened blow, the blow of the fire-snake which assumed such proportions, such executive proportions, it became the *caveat* of murder.

I would have failed to perceive it as my model crime of wishfulfilment had it not been for that ironical *caveat* – seminal thaw – which, in setting up the stoic of ambition, blew from still another quarter the waters of adventure across the face of the gorge.

That water-sermon, water-snake, blew – as the fire-snake had done – round and round, and glanced in all directions as if to retrace the mirror of unity reborn in its tracks. It was called indeed the river of soul, arose in Matope – and as is the case with many such streamers – wound its way through flags of memory across a loom of retiring fabrics, skeletons, riverbeds.

I perceived now that my red eyelid was a seal or invention on the river of the dead. A protective cover I had long misconceived, an umbrella of resources, a dug-out, a trench within the calendrical ghost of earth wherethrough the fluid elongated tear of god gathered into itself all its mythical robe or harness as sheer host of mankind, initiation of mankind, conception of unity beyond the lapse of places. The unity of long grass or feathered banks of cloud at the heart of the river. The unity of short grass or trimmed lawns of cloud in the hair of the river. The unity of heaven or sky of rapids, reflections, in feather and fin.

I would have failed again to perceive it as an inner community – an inner counsel against the solid yoke of tyranny – had it not been for those seminal rapids which, in escalating the snake of the river, blew from still another quarter across the face of the gorge. This was the landslide of Matope, and – in the beginning – when the gorge of Awakaipu was created, it sped so suddenly it seemed swifter than sermons of fire or water.

So suddenly, so swiftly I would have missed it – that landslide – been buried in it forever – were it not for the voices of fire, sermons of water which still continued far down in the mind of Awakaipu, precipitate races, Adam's races.

I could hear them now like the original accents of fear, misguided fear, thaw of mountains, flawed inventions of pride, land to water to fire.

RACES OF MATOPE

A close examination of the face of the gorge of Awakaipu reveals the path of the landslide, the path of fire, the path of water as one of the earliest pathological manifestations of races of men. That I began to see it now – to apprehend it now – was a curious omen of the medicine-man as host community: O MEN – circle of man – Awakaipu/Aesculapius. The snake that bit me had bitten its tail far back on the globe with every apparition of conquest – landslide of psychological victory and fear, race between life and death, cure and plague like the lock of god self-imposed by green man upon red. In that premature spring of the elements, bite or fang, snake or deed was conscripted into a fiend or barrier to love.

It was the deed of the race – Adam's tumbling river, Adam's cloven, land, Adam's fire – that endorsed a misguided fascination with environments of evil, polders, defences between man and man, between creature and creation.

As I began to retrace it now I was aware of this self-defeating strategy as winding and unwinding nevertheless into a subconscious thread, circular or otherwise, miraculously flawed, and therefore open to community like a subtle host of alternatives beyond a collective fiend. First I found myself on the winding staircase of the landslide.

There the earth-race lived and moved, gritty, pebbled, enclosed in the seminal rapids of the landslide, seminal flood, mask of pity.

Where my red eyelid was stood a red pebble, green eyelid a green one. I could feel the race of pebbles like a flurry of marbles in time's hand bouncing down the staircase of landslide through the sockets of god's childhood until two stuck and held there in my head. Deed of the eye, monolith of vision. It seemed disconcerting now that I had been deceived by the sleight-of-hand of a child – race or game whose flight on the staircase turned into my frieze or investiture, gorgon's marble, evil eye. It was deed or monolith I saw again that wrapped my vision round in the beginning with a conviction of evil – precipitate seal as the fiend of light.

The pebbles which rained and stuck in their sockets – in that earth-race – were of infinite susceptibility to my green and red – black or purple – crimson or pearl – summer or winter solstice. It was this ceaseless play of elongated shadow or light that carried the thread of my vision towards them so subtly, so enormously, it resembled the landslide of the moon – marble of the moon – the gambol of the tides as an unseen staircase inscribed minutely nevertheless upon each shell or stone – head or race – in relation to the sea of day or the stars of night.

It was a combination of the aim of a child and the frightened target of man that consolidated a misconception of scale – cloven staircase of maturity (half-child, half-man) – arrested species – half-fable, half-fear – weather of the gorgon. For as the pebbles raced – as god's child played its lightning hand at the top of the landslide – the piaiman bullets he let loose seemed to glance in all directions (apologetically almost, aimlessly at times) so that in inscribing their multifarious orient or compass of origins they seemed to conscript the path of the stars and the sun into ambivalent fates – a preoccupation with impersonal spaces, impending densities, punitive raids as well as a conviction of the inefficient sights of a tyrant, hiatus of storm in whose deed of calm the earth-race momentarily basked – frozen indifference.

As I peered through that seeming mask of peace, *through* that deed of calm that had once smitten me with such indifference (peered through like one who stood both within and without his shell of time) – I was aware of the pathology of eternity (landslide, fireslide, waterslide) and it seemed to me now that the gorge of Awakaipu (fistland, headland) possessed, in a transition of ages – for the first revealing time – a self-corrective void or seminal proportion as the sorrow of freedom; and the seeming randomness of the piaman's lightning hand in that context – finger of the seashore, finger of the riverbank, finger of valley or ridge – became an intimate web, thaw of space, and universal spectre of care.

SORROW OF FREEDOM

The species of the earth-race – born of the sorrow of freedom – stood, it seemed, within the self-corrective void of the staircase I had glimpsed a moment or two ago and their pebbled apparel drew them together even as it seemed to pull them apart within the piaiman's cup or fist.

I felt I could see them still in their hollow cave as in my own dreaming death shaped by the webbed hand of the medicine-man into elders of landscape – my stunned elders – greybearded children who had aged in their sleep, the deed of sleep. Sleep had, in the beginning, hit them between the eyes as they stood – each in his turn – in heaven which had revolved all of a sudden into the eerie middle or bottom of the staircase, into chopped wave, island page or continental jacket of god. As such their dreams became evil as though the elder of water (the page-child of water) had been turned into a striking mirror or jealous ageing function, and the elder of land (the page-child of land) had been fused into a conniving frame around that jealous ageing function of water mirroring the sun.

For those children or greybeards had been appointed, in turn, as the substitute hand of god to play freely, innocently, with the marble of the sun.

Their appointment occurred before they actually fell though now in tracing their pathological beard – forests of land or water – it was difficult to disentangle when they had been smitten into archaic regions.

Perhaps – in the first place – it was a forest of shadow which the page-child of water mistook for his devilish capture, mirror to palm, wave to land. As such when he fell from the very top of the staircase (from the threshold of heaven) he brought his self-deceptive cloud as the atmosphere of a prison into which he began to age without unshackling himself from mistaken capture, since he wished to preserve a link with the marble of creation he had rolled and imprinted on his hand as the lightning of sleep – god's sleep.

Perhaps – in the second place – it was the lightning in the water against him which the page-child of the land mistook for a devilish firmament. As such when he looked up to the very top of heaven he smote himself in advance – drew himself down in advance – into a captive lifeline or sun. Therefore he served but to encircle himself with the image of lightning and the shores of his earth-race remained a sleeping door or blow of freedom.

Blow to freedom. I could not be sure in the pathology of space which was nearer the truth – blow to or blow of freedom. I began my investigations afresh by entering the seminal proportions of the staircase as if these were a new kind of "go-between" – a kind of waiting room or message which I planted and shared with the elders of land and water in and on whom I stood half-reflected, half-unreflected. As much as to say that only thus could I genuinely intercept that blow as coming from one end or arising from another on the globe, and rob it thereby of inflicting the fruit of fate (stoical child of the dead) – rope or snake that bit me on Matope.

So intercept the blow that my age – the age of the dead – would perceive its dual arrest, would *see* its grey-beard institutions, helpless birthdays, year after year, century after century within the contusions of space as an intercessional wound between the unflinching child of god and the ancient scars of men.

Would see my age – the age of the dead – growing out of its prison of arrest – deed of arrest – in such a way as to become the inconspicuous seed of waking sleep (Awakaipu's sleep) which had taken a century and more to begin to sprout through red pebble, green pebble, cured vision. I stood now within the seminal tree of Matope. An elder socket of water – an elder ghost of land – fertilized its own rain of elements like a bunched grape. It was this contradictory wound – pearl of heaven – that drew me to trace abrasion or eye reflected in fallow blood as it began to sprout. So that since one eye had aged a hundred years at least since Awakaipu's bruise into Awakaipu's grape, and the other hung heavy now upon its vine of space, it was the scale of the seed that branched through my dreams as the cured gorgon of heaven (pearl beyond price falling out of my head) into a lengthening age or shadow of vision that released the fatality of the universe from an unconscious snake upon god's wrist into Awakaipu's tree of Adam.

THE CURED GORGON OF HEAVEN

It was as if – standing now outside of Awakaipu's tear diversified by the gorgon of heaven into the wealth of space – I was aware of my own primitive seed that had aged without consciousness into its own cure of memory's bite – snake of the mind. Thus it was I was able to sprout all unseeing, still seeing, remembering nothing, remembering everything through the dead pupils of the earth-race shaped by the medicine-man as he spat on the globe – self-bite, self-anguish, self-reflecting humour or gland.

I knew I had come to the strangest bitten intersection in the staircase of dreams – unfeeling anguish of rain as it poured from his side or lips or eyes as from the gargoyle of creation (architecture of Awakaipu). It was here that the fountain of space shone on one hand as the dry-eyed paradox of heaven in the city of god – red and green traffic signals – sunrise and sunset bridegroom of souls, and faded on the other hand into a body of darkness.

For such a body may well have been the original fountain in the gorge of Awakaipu – without cure or injury, traffic of substitutes, lust or marble, visionary excreta. If therefore it had seemed in a flash (that pearl or tear falling from my head) to be memory's self-bite, drought and remorse (food of the gorgon) now it darkened equally into a time prior to the glands or humours of cruel ecstasy: into a sponge for which it could be mistaken as the greedy primitive sex of god. Seminal tragedy.

As it darkened it was as if its dripping feet had been set on a path away from every hill of execution, staircase or hall or room, cross or axe, sorrow of freedom, incestuous bullet. It was this seminal sponge of ages (prior to glands or humours or awakening blood) which sipped the tears of Awakaipu afresh on Matope as a hot and scalding landslide that seemed all the more crushing because it was bottomless, peerless, sponge of annunciation – all the more devastatingly intimate because it was tangential to an art of greed – gorge of soul.

I was drawn now to follow on the trail of the sponge as upon the long-lost path I had glimpsed of the age of the rainmakers. Its dripping feet seemed both consistent and inconsistent with the age of love – the age of showers beyond sea and land.

Consistent in that its departure from every chamber of sleep or simulated execution seemed to imply features of absorption – fountain of space – fountain of compassion – like a translating agency of biter and bitten, eyelid or bait of stars, wrinkle of heaven. As such it endorsed something prior to the fluid of man or the teeth of the devil – something in itself perfect (incapable of flaw or blemish) but endlessly appearing flawed, swollen and receptive, endlessly condensing the moisture of tragedy into a new precipitation of relief, new seed, new birth.

Inconsistent however in that the contents it harnessed in this way – moist galactic feet in suspension of the dance of death – seemed to bind the trail back to a film of need (chamber of earth). And the question arose – "Did the sponge of space squeeze its own blood in appearing to drink and redress the rivers of the dead?"

It was a question of ultimate fluid responsibility which began to reverberate like thunder across the landslide of age as I contemplated the massacre attributed to me by my German ghost or employer (mediumistic river of souls) – the hand of Awakaipu – "awakener of drought".

As though it was I whose primitive archetype of fire squeezed dry the colours of pity until not a bead remained, not a green star or tear, not a red drop of blood. Nothing but rags of drought – rags of cloud like tattered races or resurrections across the centuries through which I felt as one who began to drown within generations of ambition in the antithesis of the sponge. Rags of drought. Fire-races of technology. Cloud-races of industry. I could feel the prophetic monolith of inhumanity (white painted black, black painted white) in my dead bones – the bridegroom of thunder – and I knew that the evaporation of colour in the lightning heart of the sponge had set its forge on

Matope as though to brand me afresh with my own art or block, paint or canvas.

It was this paint of fire, paint of ultimate ironic responsibility, that served to blaze through me now the question of the wound of the sun – colour of bone – I had simulated as the seal of god on the face of my people. Yet he (the medicine-man of space) could harness his flood of compassion from my drought and remorse like a miracle of antithesis – like a river of *caveats* in a desert – like the sponge or age of newborn host as I relinquished my race of heaven to the rain of nativity.

THE LAUGHTER OF THE WAPISHANAS

NOTE

In 1948 – when surveying in the upper Potaro Kaieteuran area of Guiana – I came upon a group of Wapishanas who are reputed to be a "laughter-loving" people unlike the fatalistically inclined Macusis and Arekunas.

The Wapishanas are neighbours of the Macusis and though they are said to be different in temperament they possess equally a certain decorum or ritual stiffness akin to a decoy of fate. At the time I remember making notes on the theme of laughter as the decoy of fate or vice versa.

Events within the past decade bear out the necessity for an imaginative relativizing agency within neighbouring though separate peoples whose promise lies in gateway conceptions of community.

The predicament of the Indian continues to deepen with new uncertainties as to the authority which governs him. Such authority has been at stake for centuries within the decimation of the tribes. And a political scale is still lacking: the land under his feet is disputed by economic interests and national interests. It is within this background that the theme of the decoy seems to me pertinent to the whole continent of South America. For not only does it reflect the ruses of imperialism which make game of men's lives but occupies a curious ground of primitive oracle as well, whose horizons of sensibility we may need at this time to unravel within ourselves as an original creation.

SERMON OF THE LEAF

Somewhere on the staircase of the earth-race laughter was born in the sermon of the leaf. It was a curious inexplicable birth because there were years of drought when the source of laughter itself appeared to wither on the lips of the Wapishanas. A young girl of the tribe (herself called Wapishana) dreamt one day that she now cradled the dry mourning leaf of the elder tree of laughter.

She set out with it on the staircase of drought in search of the colour and nature of laughter – the source of laughter – which she was determined to restore to the lips of her people.

It was an ancient staircase which at that moment looked as dry and brown and wooden as the mourning leaf of the elder tree of laughter. It even had branches that seemed to issue in all directions as though to simulate the age of Wapishana's people: one branch for the elder tree of bird perched faraway in the dazzling reaches of the sky, one branch for the elder tree of fish swimming faraway in the dazzling bed of sky, one branch for the elder tree of animal concealed within bird and fish, one branch for the elder tree of god...

These, amongst many other branches, seemed to quiver almost as if they knew intimately the leaf of mission Wapishana bore as she knew her own tongue against her teeth. As if to whisper (one breath to another breathlessness, one flesh to another cage or prison) that that leaf she now carried in her head, in the markings of each palm or hand, sole or foot, had sprung from them – the walking tree or limbs of laughter – in the beginning of age when the people of Wapishana came along the elder branches of fate – along the branches of hunted bird and fish, animal and god.

Wapishana held their flesh or leaf, stamped irresistibly into the root of her senses, to her lips afresh and blew along its stiff razor-like edge as if to share something of the mingling of the sharpest blow of sorrow in the strings of laughter. It was as if the withered sliced lips of her people had become the sculpture of a song – an ancient feast of the bone which sometimes turned the tables of the tree on hunter by hunted in order to memorialize a silent debt of creation – creature to creature.

Wapishana decided to take the first leg of her journey back to the source of laughter along the elder tree of bird which stretched faraway into the dazzling reaches of the sky.

ELDER TREE OF BIRD

As Wapishana made her way along this limb of the tribe she felt herself betrothed in a curious way to the spirit of the wood: puberty of the tree.

At a certain juncture her ankles and wrists seemed part of that branch – as if someone or something had grafted her there or sculpted her there into the tree of dreams: as if her thighs and breasts had been carved into a single memorial column with a knob where her forehead arched into bridge and nostrils, a crack where her lips stood from which a pointed leaf grew, tip of her tongue. It seemed almost derisory (that tip of her tongue) – tip of laughter at her own address, swaddling clothes, captive limb, bride of place.

As if the hunt of feathered species began with a joint or pact – elder bridegroom and derisory maiden – he (the elder tree) decked out with the yellow knob or beaked flame of the powis of the sun to woo her pointed sceptical leaf as a foretaste of humour – humour of bird-in-man, man-in-bird, reciprocal tongue of the psyche, marriage feast or memorial tree. She could not help laughing again at the grand air the bush turkey wore as self-sufficient decoy (powis and god, feathered man) as he approached her in solemn stiffness across or within the bough of fate. She continued to make a rude face at him – a mocking face at god – as

144

he stiffly addressed her; and the leaf she bore which sprang from his feather became razor-sharp in their joint quarrel.

This leg of her journey towards the source of laughter had reached its first memorial juice of the skeleton – bridal feather-in-leaf whose pliant quarrel drew her to taste afresh an inexplicable humour of self-mockery in self-creation – vinegar of love. She felt it now on her lips (god's kiss) – kiss of sun upon maiden of drought like acid rainfall of secrets in mourning leaf or plant, blood in stone.

Wapishana recalled the morning she set out with the sun on her lips like a silent yellow beak shorn of its crest and wings. She recalled how she seemed part and parcel of the torn fabric of space – as if she herself were the scissors of fate which constituted her horizons. So that she moved and still did not move as though her scissors and legs – inner and outer horizons – permitted her to cut the cloth of heaven into progressive and variegated shapes. As if – in addition to the sun or shorn yellow beak on her lips – the leaf or word of the dance she bore in her head had been sliced into the palm of her hand, sole of her foot, crown of her head. Each step she made therefore corresponded to inner and outer crenelations of psyche – horizons of re-entry into the movement of creation akin to an approach to the universal mate of heaven. And each landmark she gained was less a question of marching time than of alterations of horizon – legs or scissors into decoy of space or reality of the game.

The apparition of the decoy signified unsmiling summons to the elder tree of fire. The apparition of the reality of the game signified smiling advance into the elder cloud of rain. And so the two were complementary like a comedy of passion wherein – on one circle or horizon – the yellow beak, crest, claws, feathers seemed to hover as one burning creature. On another the yellow beak, crest, claws, feathers broke – each at a tangent to the other – into separate items of dew in the morning mist.

The nature of this complement (as though nature wooed nature, night day) between fire and water became the ripple of laughter within the fold of the elements – cloth or flesh or wood. She recalled the mixed brew of scorn and pity that made her laugh at herself as a trophy of marriage – a smooth column with a knob for a forehead as the defiant leaf of her tongue smote him (mate of heaven) to the tune of broken address – knob on a stick – gleaming head of maiden-phallus. Thus Wapishana felt herself to be in the shining dew of god.

It was a curious way to become conscious of the smooth breach of herself through another whose fluid stroke was akin to her own brow jointed upon phallus (her trophy of penetration) so inter-mingled as to appear both the head of another, strange to herself, and the head of one, born of herself.

Wapishana had now travelled far back or through the ritual scissors (horizons) of the tribe – the age of puberty. It was an uncanny decoy upon which she sailed and the limbs she once possessed – holy and perfect – were turning inwards and out-wards into a counter-revelation of parts that abolished the naked unselfconscious unity of the tribe. That dying unity – almost unrecognizable now as a communal mirror – served as a riddle of parts – numb comedy of man – divided source of laughter; for as Wapishana stood now on the threshold of the sliced mate of god – as she drew herself up to fly on the elder tree of bird – to spring through the open scissors of light she was aware, all at once, that something analogous had happened to her and the tribe a long time ago. Something in the nature of the leap she now wished to make. Something which had flown already from the other side of heaven through the horizons of age into her winged scissors. And as it leapt or flew then the horizons had closed – snapped shut upon her and upon it.

In closing, however, those scissors had fashioned her and saved her within the slice of memory from a timeless leap into total extinction – fashioned her and held her there (redress of death and life) to assemble a pall of rain as the gift of life.

ELDER TREE OF FISH

The second leg of her journey to the source of laughter took her along the elder tree of fish. A shower had fallen and the pool upon which Wapishana sailed was so clear she could see a cloud of fish like silver leaves in the hand of the sky. Each fish that she seized in turn settled in the palm of her hand as it fell from his (the hand of the sky) like a duplicate lifeline, duplicate sun in the water.

It was the strangest intercourse of fate – to be showered by this hand or mint – as before (upon the elder tree of bird) she had been kissed by the immanent beak of heaven and sliced by the immanent scissors of heaven.

Like a smiling, unsmiling merchant of fate – one hand wrinkling silver upon her – the other clawing gold about her – as he bargained for a style of death – plunge of the fish – maiden juice of extinction.

He had come a far way (the merchant of soul) in search of bait, scent, clue with which to beguile or redeem everything – annunciation of primitive lifeline. For this he was prepared to stake all he possessed upon an exotic *caveat* (pool of laughter).

Wapishana saw him (this merchant or bridegroom of conquest) approaching her upon the ritual staircase of god (decoy of reflection, decoy of pool) as the reification of everything – reification of juices of illusion : a reification within which one saw both the wealth and largesse of irony. It was this irony or *caveat* of nature she saw at the heart of the pool in which their reflected hands clasped, ironic lifeline of Christ, lifeline of the fish inscribed in her palm.

As with the horizons on the elder tree of bird – circle of unity on which the yellow beak, crest, claws, feathers of the sun seemed to hover as one creature – circle of dispossession on which the yellow beak, crest, claws, feathers advanced (each at a tangent to the other) like separate trophies of dew on branches of cloud – *so now* Wapishana was aware of horizons of depth akin to a lifeline of unity within her exotic grave, within the pool of wealth as the marriage portion of humanity – akin also to a landslide of greed within her exotic grave, within the rubble of wealth as wave of remorse.

So that as the merchant of soul held her (clasped her to his breast) he appeared to drown with her in all states of mankind, stone as well as flood, tyrannical or benign. To pull her down into the depths of the pool (draw her up again into every style of the paradox of death) – so that the very veil of the pool into which they plunged seemed to immure her, save her from (even as it seemed to immerse her, steep her in) extinction. Save her from death by drought as she stood within an original pall or cloud of rain.

ELDER TREE OF ANIMAL

As Wapishana made her way along the elder tree of animal she was aware of a buried arch or horizon now uplifted which had been concealed before within the elder tree of bird and elder tree of fish. It was an arch upon which, as she moved now, she became aware of sunrise at one end gradually piling up towards noon and apparently subsiding or filtering away as it descended towards the other end. And what was remarkable about this was that she began to perceive, for the first time, the progress of the tribe as a relative agent inclining to one absurd extreme or the other – absolute reification or absolute extinction. In fact that arch corresponded to a line that simulated the flight of a bird through the scissors of space or the lifeline of a fish from hand to hand upon which to measure the game of consciousness as one would collate the accumulated wisdom in the dispersal of the tribe through invitations issued by hunter to hunted – palm or summons of youth, crenellated fingers of age spread out across the sky, obverse or reverse decapitations or revolutions in the atmosphere.

Invitations which loomed on that arch as towering decoys of man looking towards sunset into which the game leapt (tall as a smouldering wall into the night): invitations which undermined those towers by looking towards sunrise across the pool of darkness into which the game leapt (inconspicuous as the seed of reality in the flare of a match).

At one end of the arch where the journey commenced along the elder tree of animal Wapishana perceived the constellation of cloud known to the tribe as the golden age of laughter. It possessed many towers fashioned like claw and beak – wrinkled claw around the eyes of the tribe – wrinkled beak upon the lips of the tribe. There was a curious subsidence in that beak and claw buried in human flesh like gold in a giant's teeth (marsh of space).

So that as Wapishana made her way through the golden age of laughter – half-sunken dawn, half-uplifted features – she felt the precariousness of her foothold, oscillations in cavern or mouth, anatomy of the feast.

Farther along the arch of the road – as Wapishana advanced and looked back – the head of the sun lay rusting now within its own mounds or mouthfuls of globe like the comedy of gold traced everywhere or the weight of laughter in bog or cosmos. And *flesh* had been engendered as this palimpsest of gold – fertility awakened as the miraculous soil of artifice. Each wrinkle or smile was the bed or track of beak and claw within the flesh of ancestor marsh or newborn swamp. Once again Wapishana was aware of every precarious leaf or foothold of sun in gigantic cities of cloud on the elder tree of animal as guarding against or being guarded by the subsidence of species.

Subsidence of species. Wapishana had the strangest sensation that every step she now took left her footprint in another's flesh so that the hardness of the globe became her self-deception akin to the merchant of soul – the decoy of soul – and the true game of reality (tender as the night) lay down the arch of the road *through* and *beyond* the purchase of extinction.

She now stood, however, somewhere in the middle of that arch (blocking the spirit of sunset) against the tower of noon, and behind her the golden age of laughter as it issued from the mouth of dawn or the rusting head of the sun seemed a kind of neolithic cloud – neolithic agriculture – comedy of the leaf. A leaf that still blew through the tower of noon like the flight of a bird or the dive of a fish until the path Wapishana took into the subjective precipitation of night seemed to echo to those footprints of beast in the thickness of air and thinness of water.

It was the thickness of air that constituted, in the first place, another's flesh of the beast in which she trod. It was the thinness of water, in the second place, that constituted another's flesh of the beast in which she trod from the beginning of time when man sold man to the elements. The tower of noon was the flesh of air. The tower of noon was the flesh of rain subtly conforming to Wapishana's footsteps in the moist places of earth as it steamed into dust or cloud equally susceptible again to the spoor of the tribe.

That spoor or footfall – in the subtlety or immateriality of tribal horizons – subsidence of globe – provided her with the first inklings of the decoy of night long before the tower of noon fell. In a sense the allure of night (the lair of the beast) had been measured for her in advance of her stride. And yet measureless it still was like a yielding substitute whose sponges were the graces of the void, the succulent mirror of god.

As she began to descend upon the sponge of air and water the reflection of noon seemed now less consistent with an absolute tower than with the sun's cap turned into a basin akin to the light footfall of space – lake in the sky – succulent mirror – lair of the fish.

And thus, slowly, increments of night were there long before night itself grew: invisible ruses of night in the crumbling dome of heaven: ruses akin to light veils – veil of lake upon fish – veil of chameleon – veil of spendthrift gravity. It was the transparent decoy of night – aerial beast – at the heart of sunrise and sunset Wapishana followed through the towering redress of noon, veils of noon. That night had already fallen under the skin of day was the most contradictory vision of the lair of the beast that turned, as it were, its own primitive decoy of the dual senses into something far in advance of the onset of nature – prior to the onset of nature – a model of original extremity unfleshed by night or day.

ELDER TREE OF GOD

And thus Wapishana came through a veil that was no veil to stand on the last leg of her journey to the source of laughter – elder tree of god – cloud or model of original extremity unfleshed by night or day.

It stood there (that cloud) at the heart of antithesis – contradictory species of darkness – contradictory species of light. Wapishana attempted to grasp it as the assembly of yellow beak, crest, claws, feathers advancing into a single creature upon her – or departing, each at a tangent to the other, into the nonexistent mate of heaven.

She attempted in the same token to visualize it as a hollow

shower or mint – maiden juice of extinction – comedy of the ironic bridegroom of the soul.

But however she looked at it it became senseless and faint except as the source of laughter – the first or the last model of man made in advance of the woman of the soil – in advance of bog or bed. As such it seemed to possess no authentic subsidence which could be verified – no sunrise, no sunset, no blood – but merely an unconscious plea that in its extremity it was the enduring laughter of the tribe which all would come to wear in death standing against drought – within another folded maiden light as veil or sap out of which the first stitch of rain would fall from the elder tree of god to tie a leaf to unfleshed wood.

ARAWAK HORIZON

Sculpture is the mind of the skeleton.
                    – Anonymous Epitaph

NOTE

Sven Loven in his Origins of the Tainan Culture, West Indies, *points out that* seme *is a true Arawak word akin to* zemi *which derives from the South American continent. In its manifestations within the Arawak consciousness* seme *or* zemi *appears to have a far-reaching sensitive role associated with poetry or sculpture which has been translated as "sweet" or "delicate".*

In some degree, I believe, "sweet" and "delicate" mirror a certain conception of frailty which makes all the more remarkable the survival of the Arawaks today in the Guianas when the fierce Caribs themselves who conquered them – long before Columbus came – have vanished in the twentieth century save for a remnant here and there.

In this story – the last in this volume – my intention is (as before) to concentrate on a personal exploration, within the late twentieth century, of vestiges of legend.

In defining this exploration as an arch or a horizon I have sought not to ring those vestiges round but to release them as part and parcel of the mind of history – the fertilization of compassion – the fertilization of the imagination – whose original unity can only be paradoxically fulfilled now through aspects of ruin or frailty within the material of consciousness through which one may begin to free oneself from overburden and stress – from fixtures and totalities – from conscriptions and races – which may have been consolidated, in the first place, as compensations of weakness.

It is in this new unshackled confessional sense, therefore, I believe – on behalf of the Other whose past or future I inhabit – that originality, coming from any source, fulfils the mind of history by participating a seminal freedom or mathematic of space arching through the prison of environment.

ONE

I dreamt I crossed the Arawak horizon at a point on the arch of space known as the mind of the skeleton where a giant sculpture rose out of ruined magma into sky-scraper day and night. Once upon a time it had been a total fire that could not be domesticated or swung away into the heavens like a great door or sun in space and it locked all men out (as tyranny of insulation) or in (as factor of extinction). Yet the key to that door fell into my hands long afterwards as I began to retrace the undreamt-of steps of the prisoner of life through the Arawak sun. Undreamt-of, that is, until now as though I too had been fashioned by metamorphoses of volcano so that my dreams of reborn fire were his late passages of darkness, my eyes enslaved to light his corridors of gloom in the mountainside through the total fire of the sun into the original sculpture of night.

Mind of night in which intensities blazed at angles of vision to participate something of hollow cavity seminal to freedom, rooms or passages illuminated by consciousness to unfold a trail of numbers – dispersal of original fugitive or fugitives from the beginning of time –O, I, 2, 3, 4, 5, 6, 7, 8, 9 articles or furnitures retraced with a child's finger in ash or sand or dust as the code of the prisoner of life locked up in the Arawak sun.

Prisoner of the sun. Room of the sun. It was a distinction of originality that brought me up with a shock as I began to apprehend the hollow eyes of landscape – once both volcanic and unbearable, unapproachable – as the visionary numeral of life.

Who would have dreamt prior to the birth of night (soil or slate of stars) that a prisoner, or prisoners, had once stood there at the heart of fire to inscribe existences of freedom within a gaol of environment? To inscribe these with a pin of light comparable to a child's X-ray in the womb – X-ray finger invoking proportions, populations, dispersals upon the slate of darkness as the sun's body swung blind and open as night?

The first prisoner to creep through the walls of fire was inscribed by the child as ○ · ○ had stood there, I dreamt, in my shoes (as I now in his or hers) within the ring of the furnace. Ring of fire which seemed to clasp him then to the breast of non-existence as it clasped me now through ash or dust, slate of numbers, soil of conception upon which to inscribe the origin of flight.

○ was the child's first sculpture – mind of the skeleton. ○ had been drawn or carved in the dust of the skyscraper like a window or bowl scooped out to signify no one and nothing and yet to suggest ironically that this record in itself – this style of vacancy – embodied a sensibility across the ages through which to re-create an arch – a journey backwards into the creation of the Arawak sun. And that journey had begun when I stumbled on to the slate of night upon which the child-factor of god had been inscribed as an omen of fire.

Child-factor or ○ . It was as if I saw now the seminal mathematic or key to the door of the sun. Door and window. Bowl of subsistence. These were the instinctive properties of the ancient Arawak sun within the newfound ash of place – palimpsest of stars created by an original prisoner.

I began to look around carefully at the furniture in the room of the Arawak sun, the bowl under the window, the stars across the threshold in the wake of the door. I knew I must acquaint myself intimately with this black/white interior as the slate of memory and the chalk of cosmos whose arch extended from primeval earth-skeleton to modem skyscraper.

The prisoner I now embodied in the skeleton of the mind had drawn a round face ○ and beneath this a stem to make ♀. I was conscious once again of the sensibility of a key with which to unlock premises of originality otherwise beyond dreams, beyond the link of participation. My creation of the room of the Arawak sun therefore possessed a stark almost undreamt-of simplicity – a round head and a stem (○ and |) that metamorphosed itself into objects in the room as if these were bound up in self-portraits of the prisoner. The key now turned into the skeleton of memory and became a table, a new item of furniture ♀ which revealed or unlocked itself within and upon the slate of night.

I lifted the bowl from the floor of the room and put it on the table and crouched before it like a man in prayer – subsistence of sun's grace. As I closed my eyes I began to embody an ancient dawning mathematic of darkened inwardness – a way of visualizing my folded limbs in the cosmos – whose first naïve Arawak inscription upon skyscraper looked like the kneeling figure of a star 2.

As I opened my eyes I was struck this time by the faceless bowl on the table like a bone in which some creature (myself) had gnawed a hole in the room of the Arawak sun. It was as if I supped now afresh on both remorse and compassion: compassion for a nameless animal I embodied and digested in the transubstantiation of numbers O, I, 2 which invoked the life that endured through and in spite of the limits of deadly environment.

I recalled that when I had first seen the bowl on entering the room it had seemed to me part and parcel of a window. And now – as I concentrated upon it – still kneeling within the skyscraper sun – that aspect (the gnaw of space) returned, and I could see, through the window of the skeleton I dreamt I embodied, a strange and extinct beast innocent of cloud. It seemed to run within a non-atmosphere, within lifeless weatherless rainless sky, as if to invoke an impossible climate upon which my gaze was now bent (forwards into the future and backwards into the past) to reconstruct upon time and space a fantasia of extinct species.

"You see," I said to myself as to the musical ghost of time, "the paint of the sun serves as a primitive long-lost equation between an inhospitable ancient fire or sound and every barren newfound stretch of wilderness. As something akin to a splinter or crackle of bone in a room or desert. Nothing may live there except in our capacity to invoke that fragment as the food of memory arching across heaven like a rift in every static circumstance. We seek therefore, in salvaging an extinct species our ancestors pursued, to arouse afresh for future ages a conception of the game of weather on the deadliest planets situated beyond earth's atmosphere in the present like a fossil plateau situated within earth's dreaming crust in the past."

I gnawed at the bone in the Arawak sun and through the window of art depicting inhospitable space as relevant to the march of science sought to trace the slenderest backbone in the sky of the strange weathered beast of god I had thought extinct. In a sense it meant reliving the buried past arching through the present into the future as an evaporation of spirit signifying an existential rainbow or mnemonic waterfall.

Where the head and stem of the prisoner of the sun had appeared before two heads now stood – a head of spirit within a head of evaporation – slate of the sun – circle within a circle ◎ rainbow within a rainbow.

But these soon readjusted themselves into a circle upon a circle making the figure 8. Then 8 was sliced in half into a flattened half-circle upon a half-circle making self-portrait 3. I turned this self-portrait of the rainbow on its bottom, arose from my knees and sat at the window like a cipher of fire ⨃. A chair began to materialize beneath the prisoner (myself) within the desert of heaven – a high-backed chair which he (or I) drew with two strokes ∟ and then embodying the tension of circles and half-circles into a single line drew himself upright on his high-backed chair as the figure 4.

It was curious but it was as if the glow of weather I sought to arouse through a waterless, primeval window had thrust its horns ⨃ into the prison of the Arawak sun as though to confirm the throned enigma of life. Would a maggot of rain spring from the anatomy of colours I embodied like a worm uncoiling itself for the first time in the drought of heaven? Or was this uncanny meat of rain – maggot of fertility – a witness of something apparently self-engendered but in reality *other* than premises of primeval corruption? Would the worm of rain come to signify something beyond its own atmosphere – something akin to a black star of life or ultraviolet slate?

These were the questions that had been unlocked by the subjective/objective key to the room of the sun. In the same way that I grew aware of horns of weather as my base of anatomy like a sliced 8 ⨃ turned on its curved bottom or side, so I was conscious now – as I sat at the window looking out as well as in – of the tail or brush of the cosmos plunging in the wake of its horns where my flesh was enthroned within the prisoner of constellations.

TWO

The tail of constellations – half-web, half-vacancy – that swept the room was now an original blowing arch that seemed to embody bowl U and chair L akin to a portrait of the sun 5 (upside down shadowy chair and sideways half-lit bowl). The wind sweeping through the room turned the stars and articles within into a fantasia of reconstruction like a musical score. The prisoner himself who had long been freed as opus of fire seemed now both rooted and aligned to bowl and chair 5 like anamnesis of a dance which stood him on his head – arched back (bowl), bent knees, horizontal feet (chair).

Thus it was the evaporation of spirit became the genesis of freedom in furniture of arousal like self-portraits of wind as if a great theme of flight were at the heart of architectural motifs across the ages – architectural malaise – nostalgic periods, restoration of idols – solipsistic tenancy.

The window of Arawak skyscraper at which I now sat in the musical chair of the prisoner of old seemed bent in the eye of a storm 6 like a curious maggot of vision or whirlpool or cycle of reflections blasting all complacency. It was the tail of fire uncoiling and coiling afresh around me into substitute existences or crumbling lights and walls of other existences (anamnesis of creation 7).

At first I wondered whether 7 was a child's copy or tracing of genesis (innocent restatement of whirlpool sex or 6). 7 embodied a simple vertical stroke (prisoner's bar or body) drawn thus I and a simple horizontal beam or erection drawn thus ▬ which turned in all directions 7 or Γ. But on closer fiery reflection or deeper consideration of 6 (coil of space) and 7 (marriage to

space) I was conscious of something non-derivative, non-naturalistic in the revolution of earth-skeleton into skyscraper – the
tail of vanishing prehistory into the arousal of metamorphosis.

"What do you mean by non-naturalistic?" ⅂ and Γ said to me
and (as wind and fire blew) they drew together into a joint signal
like a child's star or the wingspan and thrust of an ambivalent
flying machine in the Arawak unconscious 𐤠.

"By non-naturalistic," I said in order to humour ⅂ and Γ
within a diaspora of elements 𐤠, "I mean the breakthrough of
original dimensions – seminal re-discovery *(zemi* or *seme)* rather
than a derivative escape route into the past. I mean the living
genesis of the cornerstone of time involving and revolving within
the light of creation rather than cloaked in furnishings or ranks
which imprison us as total models of the sun. I mean the signature
of the original prisoner of life whose mathematic of otherness
(death translating life, life death) is the *caveat* of freedom without
which we are doomed to reproduce uniform environments of
hate and to hanker after romantic 'green' substitutes we reinforce
or bind into tautological nature – gaol or fortress."

⅂ and Γ were grimly laughing like the blackened limbs of the
prisoner of old – *caveat* of fire – in halfway house to the cross or
the tree †.

"Creation", I continued, "is a non-derivative balance of resources and therefore it is involved in a breakthrough from a
purely formal pattern (or deed of materialism) into a primitive/
scientific cosmos beyond civilization's end-products (end-products of hate or punitive love)."

At last the full implications of my penetration of the Arawak
sun (metamorphoses of the game of weather) were becoming
clear. I was involved in the breakthrough of an original prisoner of life from metaphorical deadly furnace or total green
nature (from insane obsessional age or idealistic crime of
youth). As though – in order to distinguish between creations
and models, the law of spirit and the execution of the deed,
genesis and earth – I needed to experience a devolution of
space intrinsic to rooms of otherness: intrinsic to the music of
rain beyond the roof of the skies. The skyscraper of man
embodied a motif of evaporation pointing to the drought of

stars as to dry rain (unearthly ruin of space) in advance of a ceiling of water or mask of heaven.

As such – in both ceiling and breakthrough – I was involved in the flight of the prisoner of god (in his vacant room or primitive dome) as in a new epic of the elements beyond the worship of nature. I was involved in the bowl of creation to which I turned now as to the receptacle of the prisoner, dry rain (unearthly ruin) upon which he supped – the seminal digestion of a bone of water by the prisoner of god in advance of cloud or model.

The gnawed bone or bowl of space stood on the table of the Arawak skyscraper like this ∪. I was aware, as I supped, of another bowl I had previously overlooked in my inventory of the stars and furnitures in the room: another bowl to imply there had been someone else to bear the prisoner company or to suggest that even then long, long ago he knew I would come and thus he proffered me the core of his hospitality *in my absence* as I supped now with him *in his.* Sitting there now I knew he and I had been created in the beginning before I materialized within his imagination of night or he dematerialized within my imagination of day.

The proxy bowl of creation had been turned down on the table thus ∩ and on an impulse I raised it and placed it upon mine like this 8 to invoke the fire of rain from hollow to hollow by rubbing dry bones together. As I scraped and pressed rim to rim, receptacle to receptacle, the Arawak horizon was sealed into the conjunctive vision of the prisoner of god 8 eighth day of the spectacles of creation ∞ skeleton of rain and light of construction.

I felt now I was half-assembling, half-groping towards or into something related to an immense witness of an evaporation of spirit (flight of god) as I supped with the prisoner in the conjunctive horizons of a primitive/ scientific cosmos. I put his spectacles on me like articulate inner/outer bones (seminal match or digestion of features) and the tail of the stars on the floor of the skyscraper suddenly threaded my eyes like the teeth of a saw – molars or millstones of god – visionary ground of consciousness within the jaw of the Arawak sun.

What sort of creation, self-made carpenter of life (my brain reeled at the flight of origins) had he been? His tail arched and still did not arch (web and vacancy): his jaw of stars traced (and still did not trace) the game of weather. His horns were the anatomy of music. Had he possessed visionary teeth (eye-teeth) of a kind of relative cutting splendour – the *saw* or mathematics of a family of suns? Had he made himself – in order to fall into himself – into the furnace of nature? Had he cut the doors of night (the black doors of space) – in order to fall out of himself – out of the furnace of nature?

And as he fell – had he framed the fire of revolutions – mother of light – mistress of darkness? "YES and NO," he replied over the rim of his bowl upon which was distilled a child's drawing of night and day as the roast of rain on which I supped – goddess of fertility; planted her breasts and made her womb ༐ shaped a triple *zemi* of cloud in the roof of the Arawak sun.

Thus began the curious feast of otherness – within-ness to without-ness – which characterized a fall into and out of the goddess he framed – conception of primitive reason – evaporation of primitive reason – match of seasons.

Tall and short were the teeth of the rain as earth-skeleton arched into skyscraper.

THREE

First I clambered upon the tall teeth in the jaw of god as though I had changed places with the roasted rain and found myself in process of being eaten by another rather than in process of eating another. My window or environment as I climbed was barred like ivory; ivory rain. And I dreamt that these bars were a fertile prisonhouse (genes of penetrance) forked cruelty of god, match of nature like blue blood upon the ivory roof of the sun.

It was this sheen or illusion that imprinted itself upon me as a total mask of effects – blue dome, ivory jaw – a total capacity with which to rake the elements in the name of skyscraper clown, skyscraper colony, skyscraper superman, skyscraper underling. The tall teeth of environment supped upon me as if I had been designed the lowliest of creatures – roasted rain in the jaw of ivory rain: roasted sun in ivory sun. And this frame of subjective dominance became my first volcanic mirror, deadly romantic gaol or order of hierarchical crime, my first model illusion of the original body of creation. Arawak of the beanstalk. Tall Jack-tooth (Jackboot) of rain. On that arch or giant tooth – reaching up to indentations of appetite as well as down to the spoor of the tribe – I waited for the jaw of god to close upon me, and as it did so the blue dome of illusion, the ivory footfall of the rain turned red as the underbelly of the sea – volcanic Arawak legend of the body of god through which the sun was on fire as it set.

It was my imagination of night that the throat of god became black like soot – black dome of earth instead of blue. As though my roasted rain – rain of my blood – had filled the mouth of god almost to overflowing. And swept me now into a deeper tide – footfall of gloom – that had spanned the sun. I could hear nevertheless, even as I thought I would be kicked up or cast down, the bars of weather clash shut behind me to frame the wind, to frame a breath on the fiery sea of space: bottleneck heaven and hell.

Slowly, as I continued to climb up (or was it down?) genetic beanstalk or black tooth of the sun, I waited for the jaw of god to open again as it had closed upon me a little while ago. I wondered if, in opening, it would let me fall back into the bowl on the table upon which the prisoner supped. And if, in thus falling back – falling out of the pit of night into the pit of day – I would have discovered the origins of fertility, the inconspicuous origins of the goddess of fertility, as a strange reflective morsel held on the tongue of the pit against the teeth of the pit, then on the lips of the pit to moisten another's tongue, against another's teeth, upon another's lips. I would have discovered the very delicacy, the *zemi* of sweetness, the rarity of communication *through* the bars of the pit – the pit of environment.

Tall and short were the teeth of the rain as I dreamt of myself in a reflective morsel, smouldering kiss of the pit (lips of famine to lips of plenty). First I remembered I had climbed the giant's tall tooth; now it seemed as I waited for the jaw to reopen I slid on to a stump. On this stump – traced by the tongue of the pit – I discerned within the grave of night what seemed to me the sculpture or footprint of a fallow deer 𝌀 drought deer in the mouth of space.

I knew I must fly with it; spring with it; voyage from the tongue of the pit. So that in the giant kiss of night and day I would stumble upon as well as leap through the giant void. And in this inner/outer devouring trail of another complex of personality which I tasted, and through which I was tasted myself by the other, I began to *see* something of the evaporation of god, flying spirit-deer, spirit-rain, spirit-fire whose arch of space repudiated a total paradise as prejudicial to the wraith of man upon a trail of *caveats* – fallow tooth (footprint) of the ghost of oneself – a self one dreams as wholly consumed in the jawbone of gods/goddesses through which one leaps to scale freedom.

FOUR

I dreamt I had discovered in my Arawak cosmos a child's drawing 8 turned sideways into the drought footprint of a deer ⋈. Spirit-deer, absent rain-deer which reshaped itself now into one remaining circle and one open line or tangent ꝗ that later slid out into the tail of the sun ꝗ.

I began to grope afresh into the waif of god or ninth day of the prisoner of life whose self-portrait I embodied across the ages at the tail of the sun: dying race, flying sun. As though I saw myself anew with distant single eye, handle of premises, baton of relays within an architecture of music or spine of rain. I saw myself far back in the sound of space, in the jaw of space – circle of peril where he (I) stood, poised to run.

That poise or threshold was the strangest expenditure of himself like the pace of the wind or the stroke of a wave to reconceive me long afterward. It was his breath of dancing consciousness prior to my self-portrait of the birth of music, the sound of rain. I saw him then as the inner paradox of myself – the very breath or arousal of my elements. I could see a deep pool of reflection like a furnace as though he invoked my fearful contradiction: superior fury/inferior frame: man as the frame of god: water as the ring of fire, earth as the footstool of heaven.

"When he flew," I asked myself, "did he die to manifest me as his compensation of life, when he ran did he fall to provide me with contours of endurance, when he stood still did he grow unconscious to embalm my station of nature as his promissory note of god, covenant of god?"

The riddle of my self-portrait had barely flooded my senses

when I saw what seemed to me compensatory witnesses or features of the evaporation of god, the ninth day of heaven.

First he had flown into the wind and in order to compensate his invisibility through me, the invisibility of the wind, had turned the objects in the room of the sun round and round into self-portraits of music, self-portraits of the falling themes of spiritual consciousness.

It was as if – prior to flying into the wind, prior to the creation of the invisible wind – he (I) stood at the door or window of the sun on the very edge of a precipice. Nothing moved since the wind had not yet simulated itself into my limbs as waif of man $\wedge$ or $\dagger$. Nothing moved until space became ivory as an antediluvian cloak in one light, grey stone or fossil goatskin in another light, blue-black wood or primitive painted canoe in still another light. Hard bleak fleet of appearances whether ivory or grey or black – as though space began to portray itself as the savage compensation of his death the instant he leaped and I was drawn. Drawn to the gravity of his theme through which the lights of space were assembled in me: drawn to the spirit of his motion through which the canoe of space enveloped me.

It was this gravity I entreated as it cloaked me now with his flight. There it was – cloak of gravity – sky-scraper canoe or tower – glazed here, diamonded there with splinters from his abyss which stared at me; splintered address I was conscious of as something prior and open to my self-portrait of the wind – something in the nature of an economic capacity to witness of him when I blew across the walls of my skyscraper. And I knew that when I painted his flight, when I conceived myself falling and being crushed anew into a savage assembly of lights, *when I dreamt it was I who fell and died,* I saw through his abyss of gravity. I SAW THROUGH HIS ABYSS OF GRAVITY. One day that towering abyss or frozen savage skyscraper of god I drew as my self-portrait would fall in its turn and drift into another's consciousness or location of dead colour on the wall of the sun. One day it would stand watching him. The next it would fall watched by him. Thus a perspective or corridor of witnesses would extend beyond self-portrait of paradox to self-portrait of paradox like death witnessing to the colours of death or the subtlest breakthrough in the endless compositional rhythms of life.

That perspective was the theme of the wind (precession of architectures) in which objects became self-portraits of flight – towers became hollow shafts – economic wings to an apparently falling theme of shared spiritual origins: thus did he (I) begin to visualize and create a body of wealth, the evolution of consciousness as bars of sound, impact of music, doors and windows of skyscraper canoe: superior flight/inferior frame in the opus of the incarnations of god.

I (he) flew into the architecture of music. He (I) created the painted sound of flesh and blood like a long train of infinite objects in whose prior native abyss I (he) dreamt it was spring, the spring of achievement.

FIRST THEREFORE HE (I) HAD FLOWN INTO THE SCULPTURE OF THE WIND...

Second he ran into the heart of vision and in order to compensate the brightness of immateriality had turned the objects in the room into self-portraits of light – incandescent theme of spiritual consciousness which began to darken into milestones and monuments.

Thus – looking back at the furnace of the Arawak sun – I saw it now as one of his first black milestones or witnesses to a theme of vision threaded to the evaporation of fire, death of fire, rebirth of fire.

It was a hard economic monument to bear – to look back upon as I dreamt I sped with his winged feet into the night. He had run and died to all intents and purposes and the cold blaze of the sun in his wake seemed mournfully and blissfully unaware it had addressed him as bank or temperature before he ran and flew.

It dawned on me now that the first black door to open in a poem of fire was a spark of recognition in the colours of the blind – blind fire to blind water – black priority to blazing priority – like the death of fire dislodging itself from every monument into a runway of vision. THUS IT WAS IN THE SECOND PLACE HE SURRENDERED HIMSELF TO THE THEME OF LIGHT AS MANIFESTED IN THE IMPACT OF FURIES, HOT AND COLD GIANT KISS OF SELF-PORTRAITS OF ATTRITION ON THE WHEELS OF NIGHT

AND DAY, GAIN AND LOSS, BLACK AND WHITE GHOST OF
OCEANIC PREMISES.

In the third place he grew still and in order to compensate a loss of
movement, or unconsciousness of movement, he embalmed the
drought of nature as the promissory note or covenant of god,
economics of rivers, evaporation or impending cosmic fall.

Thus – looking back like the ghostly composer/painter/
rainmaker of contours of the void – I saw him as my besieged
ironical tower, manifestation or bank of premises. Like someone
conscripted by the gorgon of the sun – someone whose steady
weight served as the most alien shore or extremity of love at the
heart of my gentlest oceanic folk. Milestone of Arawak survival
across the seas of soul.

It was a bitter economic lighthouse to bear – that once a
furnace of environment like the icy grip of hell had invested the
prisoner of life. And that it seemed feasible to dream no one or
nothing could have lived there at all, neither within in the heat nor
without in the cold of such a whirlpool of ice or fire, save a farflung spark of consciousness which intimated – in that breakthrough from no one and nothing (ice and fire) – that the survival
of anyone and anything, after all, upon the earth was explicable in
paradoxes or self-portraits of spiritual themes. The self-portraits
of the invisible wind – theme of frosted music, glittering hail or
sparks of dew – were dancing objects or furnitures in space. The
self-portrait of immaterial light – theme of vision – was an ironic
salutation of the blind colour of sun to the blind colour of water
in preserving as well as energizing an explosion of consciousness.
The self-portrait of mathematics – theme of absent numbers –
was an ultraviolet slate of stars. So, too, in the embalmed fortunes
of nature lay the theme of ironic perfection – freedom's fortress
of perfection and immortality as an evaporation of spirit signifying someone beyond a circumstantial bier or antithesis of breath
witnessing to every vanished life.

I looked back as I ran and flew with a sense of curious awe at the
embalmed breathless vistas of earth as models of ironic perfection. In the glaze of distance those vistas may have been parchment of fire or parchment of flood. As parchment of fire earth

171

seemed a perfect dead seal on all things. As parchment of flood earth seemed equally perfect, equally sealed or model of deadly environment. But now I perceived in that glaze of primeval distances the irony of god implicit in the flight of the prisoner: I perceived myself as an interface of elements which was both the antithesis of the seal of fire or water as well as the ceaseless mystery or breakthrough of creation into consciousness. A breakthrough which seemed in some ways the comedy of creation – antithesis of the economics of stasis, antithesis of the stasis of immortality.

I looked back as I ran and flew at the stasis of immortality (frame of god) as my most macabre outpost of the imagination where the art of self-sufficiency was so entrenched (embalmed fire or embalmed flood) that it glistened with an unconscious opposite apparition like the glazed eye of water searching for fire or the glazed eye of fire searching for water, breathlessness searching for breath. It was this glaze which now became the soul or mirror of space witnessing for the themes of the prisoner of creation in the room of the Arawak sun.

I looked forward now as I ran and flew, with the sense that in visualizing these mirrors ∞ (spectacle of fire, spectacle of water) as self-portraits of breath allied to breathlessness, I was involved in the curious reversal of the stasis of immortality into winds of fortune. As a consequence the economics of immortality, which was earth, turned round and round as my self-portrait, fortunate music, wealth of comedy I inherited from space as an upside down chair and sideways laughing bowl 5 acrobatic water.

The sun also turned round and round as my self-portrait or fortunate paint, acrobatic fire, whose arch was the wealth of divinity I inherited from space, tail of my Arawak cosmos 9 signposting the spine of the wind in the stars – treasury of The Rainmaker.

As he (The Rainmaker) ran and flew – looked back, looked forward – he was aware of himself as signifying losses therefore embodying gains in a self-portrait of the currency of time; signifying a fall therefore embodying a rise in the self-portrait of the hill of time; signifying invisible themes therefore embodying a visible frame or self-portrait of the comedy of time; signifying an evaporation of spirit therefore embodying a precipitation of life as winds of fortune blowing on every horizon or wilderness of suns.

ABOUT THE AUTHOR

Wilson Harris was born in 1921 in New Amsterdam in British Guiana, with a background which embraces African, European and Amerindian ancestry. He attended Queen's College between 1934-1939, thereafter studying land surveying and beginning work as a government surveyor in 1942, rising to senior surveyor in 1955. In this period Harris became intimately acquainted with the Guyanese interior and the Amerindian presence. Between 1945-1961, Harris was a regular contributor of stories, poems and essays to *Kyk-over-Al* and part of a group of Guyanese intellectuals that included Martin Carter, Sidney Singh and Ivan Van Sertima. His first publication was a chapbook of poems, *Fetish*, (1951) under the pseudonym Kona Waruk, followed by the more substantial *Eternity to Season* (1954) which announced Harris's commitment to a cross-cultural vision in the arts, linking the Homeric to the Guyanese. Harris's first published novel was *Palace of the Peacock* (1960), followed by a further 23 novels with *The Ghost of Memory* (2006) as the most recent. His novels comprise a singular, challenging and uniquely individual vision of the possibilities of spiritual and cultural transcendence out of the fixed empiricism and cultural boundedness that Harris argues has been the dominant Caribbean and Western modes of thought.

Harris has written some of the most suggestive Caribbean criticism in *Tradition the Writer and Society* (1967), *Explorations* (1981) and the *Womb of Space* (1983), commenting on his own work, the limitations of the dominant naturalistic mode of Caribbean fiction, and the work of writers he admires such as Herman Melville.

Following the breakdown of his first marriage, Harris left Guyana for the UK in 1959. He married the Scottish writer Margaret Burns and settled in Chelmsford. Thereafter, until his retirement, Wilson Harris was much in demand as visiting professor and writer in residence at many leading universities.

Wilson Harris was knighted in 2010. He died in March 2018.

ALSO BY WILSON HARRIS IN CARIBBEAN MODERN CLASSICS

Heartland
ISBN: 9781845230968; pp. 96; pub. 2009; £7.99
With an introduction by Michael Mitchell.

Zechariah Stevenson, son of a wealthy businessman, is the watchman at a timber grant deep in the Guyanese interior. In flight from the scandal of a fraud and the connected disappearance of his mistress, Stevenson isolates himself in the forest, which he discovers is disturbingly alive and conscious. In this vulnerable state old certainties crumble. But he is guided by three ghostly revenants from Harris's previous novels: Kaiser who has become the storekeeper of the heartland; Petra a pregnant Amerindian woman and Da Silva, the pork-knocker, whose second death points Stevenson in the direction of a journey that crosses the boundaries between life and death. Harris, who was for many years a surveyor in the Guyanese hinterland, creates a powerfully physical sense of the complex relationship between the human and the natural worlds.

The Eye of the Scarecrow
ISBN: 9781845231644; pp. 112; pub. 2011; £8.99
With an introduction by Michael Mitchell

An unnamed diarist, writing in London, in 1963, reflects on episodes of his life in British Guiana that profoundly altered his vision and understanding of the world. There are childhood incidents, such as time he pushed his friend into a canal, but finds no blame is attached to his role; there is his youthful witnessing of a march of workers in 1948, protesting the killing of their comrades by the police during a bitter strike, and his momentary, but disconcerting perception that his friend is an empty scarecrow of a man, a vision that leaves him with "a curious void of conventional everyday feeling."

There begins a radical exploration of the indeterminacy of memory and the capacity of the imagination to see beyond the everyday, to tap into the interplay between the material and the spiritual, the conscious and unconscious mind. Though Harris challenges the reader by removing the props of linear narration, he compensates by offering a poetic richness of sensuous association.

The Ascent to Omai
ISBN: 9781845233549; pp. 134; pub. 2018; £8.99
With an introduction by Michael Mitchell

Wilson Harris's ninth novel, first published in 1970, is a work of the most revolutionary and far-reaching kind of science or speculative fiction. In it time and space are truly elastic, so that events in recent time become part of remote geological time and the boundaries between events and remembering, individual persons and different locations are fluid and permeable. Victor is in search of his father, Adam, once a revolutionary worker who was sent to prison many years ago for burning down the factory he worked in. Since then Victor has lost touch with him, but suspects he is living as a pork-knocker (gold prospector) in the remote Cuyuni-Mazaruni district of Guyana – now the site of one of the largest open-cast goldmines in the world and the site of immense environmental degradation. Prophetically, the clash between the material/technological and the primordial/spiritual is one of the intercutting themes of the novel, connecting to the El Doradean myth so central to the Guyanese imagining.

As he climbs in search of his father, Victor both revisits his past relationship with him and replays his father's trial, which also becomes his own, in a way that echoes the "Nighttown" episode of Ulysses, though unlike Bloom's. Victor's offences are not sexual, but represent blockages in the openness of his thinking. Victor's search is for spiritual grace, for the compensations of love and the glimmerings of a true understanding of the world he exists in, though Harris refuses to "impose a false coherency upon material one had to digest" and the reader is invited to share in Victor's struggling ascent to consciousness, knowing that it can never be other than provisional.

All Peepal Tree titles are available from the website
www.peepaltreepress.com
with a money back guarantee, secure credit card ordering
and fast delivery throughout the world at cost or less.

Peepal Tree Press is the home of challenging and inspiring literature from the Caribbean and Black Britain.

Contact us at:
Peepal Tree Press, 17 King's Avenue, Leeds LS6 1QS, UK
Tel: +44 (0) 113 2451703 E-mail: contact@peepaltreepress.com